My Summer

of Hate

Evan Jacobs

Burning Bulb

PUBLISHING

My Summer of Hate
By **Evan Jacobs**

Burning Bulb Publishing
P.O. Box 4721
Bridgeport, WV 26330-4721
United States of America
www.BurningBulbPublishing.com

Paperback Edition ISBN: 978-1-964172-49-1

Table of Contents

Chapter 1

I never really hated anyone until the summer of 1997. I had lived in the same city of Fountain Valley, CA since I was four. Fountain Valley is in Orange County. It's located near Huntington Beach and Costa Mesa which are next to areas like Newport and Laguna Beach. Except for Fountain Valley and Costa Mesa, those places are considered beach towns. North of that are more urban areas like Santa Ana, Anaheim and Fullerton. Those cities are part of Orange County, but you wouldn't know it by how people talk about the place. You would think it's sunny all year long, girls are bouncing around in bikinis and that it's strictly White and Republican. Now, while Orange County certainly has its fair share of that, it also has its share of diversity. I didn't really start noticing this until that year. For as long as I could remember, none of the outside "cultural forces" seemed like they could touch it. I thought of O.C. (the short name for Orange County) like everyone else. Sure, we would get some occasional graffiti, or maybe a car full of lowriders would drive through my neighborhood, but that was about it.

Then out of nowhere, there started being more graffiti on the walls in Stonecress Park (which was only a few minutes from my house). More Asians started cruising around the streets driving lowered rice rockets (their tricked-out cars that my friends and I called "shopping carts" because that's what the long fins on the back of them makes them look like), and then there were the Blacks. None had ever lived around me before. Not that I minded, or at least I didn't think I would mind living around them. For the first time it seemed like I was noticing things about people I had never noticed before. More importantly, I was noticing the differences.

What follows now is the story of that summer. A period of three months that, for a lot of people, is probably better off forgotten. I don't know if my story is 100% accurate; I just know what I remember and what I think happened. I mean, this is a story, right? In looking back at that summer, I've even added some things, talks mainly, that I think probably happened behind my back, as I couldn't be everywhere at once.

This is the story of that summer. My summer of hate.

I'm a straight-edge, hardcore guy. Basically, I don't drink, smoke or do any drugs. Some think straight edge people don't eat meat, but I do, and some also think straight edge people don't have sex, which I definitely do. I just only have it with my girlfriend, Erika Lopez. She's Mexican but she doesn't look like it. In fact, when we first met I didn't know what she was until she told me. Then I went to her house and I met her parents and it all made sense. Different cultures just do things differently. Her house wasn't too different from mine but it was different enough. The biggest thing I noticed was the furniture. For example, Erika's parents had these really old, antique-looking couches, and the ones in my parents house seemed to be switched out every five years.

I play guitar in a hardcore band. Hardcore music is like a hybrid between punk rock and heavy metal. At least that's how I see it. We're not dirty and crusty like some punks, in fact to look at us you might think we were part of some sort of athletic team. A lot of us wear our hair really short. Some people shave their heads while others shave their heads bald. We wear clothes that are much too large for us, hooded sweatshirts, big khakis, skater-type shoes (I can't skate), etc. I keep my hair pretty short. I don't have any tattoos but some of the members of my band do.

My band is called Augmented. We're really big locally and we have a CD out. It just came out on a local label called Pushing Forth Records. It's run by Isaac Myles. Everyone likes Isaac. He's a rad guy but sometimes we joke, not to his face of course, that the only reason so many people in the scene like him is because he's Black. I say this because there aren't too many Black people in the hardcore scene. I don't think there's really any in the Orange County scene. Anyway, my band is popular. We sell out almost all the places we play. Carlo Riley, the singer, is a great frontman. The crowd really loves him. When we play it's like he holds them captive and they don't even know it. Carlo is my best friend. I've known him since we were in kindergarten, so I really know him and sometimes it's hard for me to be objective and see him how other people do. Especially, our bass player Russ Franklin and our drummer Adam Cranston.

I have to admit, I was pretty impressed when Carlo first started coming to practice with a notebook full of lyrics and he could actually sing. He can also play guitar too but when we started the band he wanted to sing, and since I can't (and don't want to), it made sense that I would play guitar. Carlo even came up with the name of the band. It means "greater than perfect" or something close to that. We just thought it sounded cool. Like that's the name a hardcore band would have.

Hardcore music is pretty aggressive and most of our songs are fast, but we also play some heavier sounding stuff (I'm actually trying to write more of it; I write most of our songs). Carlo can scream really well but his voice is also melodic (that's what I meant by he could actually sing). Musically though you have to watch things because in hardcore, if you slow down your sound too much, if it becomes too heavy or too melodic, people will accuse you of selling out.

Russ, Carlo and I are all 20. Adam is 16 and he just started playing drums a few years ago but he's really good. For a kid his age and his size (he's about 5'6" and weighs 120 lbs) he really hits hard.

So I play guitar and that's all I wanna do. I'm in school and I work part-time but all I think about (aside from Erika) is Augmented. Our record has sold almost 2,000 copies and its only been out for two weeks. Some people wonder if Isaac rips off his bands because he makes a living from his label and the bands don't really make anything. I don't think he does. We haven't made any money on

Pushing Forth Records but he pays for our recordings and puts our records out. That's what is most important to me, getting the music out to the people that want to hear it. Also, Isaac's label is the biggest one in the hardcore scene. There's other hardcore labels across the country and around the world (I think the second biggest hardcore label is New Dawn on the East Coast), but none of those labels are nearly as big as Pushing Forth Records. People buy stuff from this label just because it has the Pushing Forth name on it.

The way things are shaping up, Augmented is becoming an even bigger band. Maybe the biggest band in hardcore, or at least the biggest one in Orange County. And for right now that's all that matters; my band and the Orange County hardcore scene. I didn't realize it then, but this was the best time. I had my band and the safety net of going to school. I had just finished up all my general education courses at Orange Coast College with a 3.8 GPA. I didn't realize with each passing moment that I was coming closer to having to make a choice between my band and school.

Chapter 2

"Ladies and Gentlemen," Carlo said into the mic before our set that night at Club Royale. "It's summertime and we are Augmented!" The crowd cheered loudly. "This is the title song off our brand new album on Pushing Forth Records. It's called 'All the Way Back' and I want you

to sing it with me!!"

Russ smiled at me right before I started playing the opening chords to our first song. I play out of a Marshall amp using a Charvel guitar. I'm not too good with the technical stuff (Russ even has to help me tune sometimes!) but I'm getting better. I can't put it into words really, I can only say that I know how I like things to sound. There's a certain energy about hardcore music, even when it's played slow, that I don't hear anywhere else.

As soon as I start playing, Adam follows after me on the drums and Russ comes in as well. He doesn't practice his bass as much as he should but he is really talented. In fact, before I joined the band, he and Carlo had already recorded four songs on a 4-track recorder with Russ playing all the bass, drum and guitar parts. That's pretty much how the band came together so quick. We just learned those songs and then I started writing stuff. Shortly after that, Russ found Adam through a friend. It's funny because none of us had ever taken a drama class in high school or anything.

In fact the last thing I ever thought I would love would be getting up in front of people and performing, but I do. I don't know if I would like it so much if I had to do it by myself, but with Carlo, Russ and Adam there, I don't mind it at all.

Carlo and I got into hardcore at the same time. He was friends with this guy Benji Walker who is 3 years older then us. At age 15, Benji's brothers got him into punk and then Benji got Carlo into punk (Carlo kind of looks up to him), which means he got me into punk as well. Since Benji could drive he started taking us to shows, but he soon lost interest in most of the bands. He still listens to some of them but he started drinking a lot and began to make fun of Carlo for still being straight edge. So this left Carlo and I to fend for ourselves. A lot of the punk shows were happening in Los Angeles and there was no way we could get our parents to drive us there. So, we started going to the few local shows that we could find. And the only local shows happening in any kind of a vicinity to where we lived (that weren't 21 and over) were mostly straight edge, hardcore shows. We'd go and see bands like No Response or Killed Existence, and what made us keep coming back wasn't really the music but the singers for all these bands. The frontmen. They really knew how to talk. They spoke about being "there for the music" and helping people who needed help.

As time went on and we got a little older, Carlo and I wanted to be on stage and when we finally got there, all we did was imitate those guys. But by that time, the people that we were imitating had fallen out of the scene for whatever reason, so there was really nobody to call us out for what we were doing. The only people left were those who had been there when we started going to shows, but there weren't enough of them to make a lot of noise. Plus, them seeing people their own age on stage probably made them like us more. It was as if Augmented was their band.

When we play, songs in our set just flow right into the next one. A lot of bands stop in between and tune or something, but we usually don't do that until four or five songs into our set. Carlo usually talks over it so that nobody really notices that that's what we're doing. The stage (we mostly play on stages but there are times when we play on the floor if there isn't one in the club or we're playing at someone's house) is usually set up in such a way that the heads in the crowd come up to Carlo's chest. For some reason Club Royale, the club we always play in Fullerton, always puts a mic on a stand for Carlo. He always begins the set by taking the stand and putting it behind Adam. During our set, Carlo moves all over the stage, and the crowd, especially the people pressed up to the front, follow after him in a wavelike motion. Bodies seem to fly from all directions as some of the crowd circle pits, and others mosh in place, flailing their arms and doing dances that look like something out of Mr. Miyagi's Karate class. A lot of times, Carlo will just hold the mic out to the crowd and they'll sing entire songs that way. He doesn't even have to move. Russ and I joke that when he does that it's because he's "tired" or "becoming an old man."

I looked out into the audience and saw Isaac in the back of the club with the Pushing Forth Records Banner behind him. There were a bunch of people in front of the booth that he's running with his girlfriend Shayna. They're both a little older than almost everyone at the show but you can tell that they love this music. Isaac always sets up a nice booth. You'd be surprised how many people he'll have there at one time. You would think they were just going to steamroll over him but it never happens.

I turned to the side of the stage (I stopped having to look at the frets on my guitar I don't know how long ago) and saw Deborah and Lisa. Those are Russ' and Adam's girlfriends. Deborah and Russ are perfect for one another because they both have big mouths. Sometimes I wonder how they stand each other but they've been together for over four years.

Then I see Erika looking at me. She's beautiful. That's honestly what I think every time I look at her. It's summer so she's wearing an orange tank-top and a white skirt. She's easily the prettiest girl at Club Royale and I'm not saying that just because she's my girlfriend. You can tell when people look at her that they realize they're seeing somebody special. She smiles and I smile back. It's nice when the people you care about know how important something is to you. It's almost like it can become equally important to them.

I turned toward the band again. Without even thinking about it, we transition into our next song.

Chapter 3

Going to 7-11 after a show always feels great. The owner of Club Royale likes to turn up the heat really high so that kids will buy more sodas (which probably makes them even more thirsty). He only gives one bottle of water to each member of each band, so every time I leave a show that I play there, I feel dehydrated. It felt good just walking into 7-11, even though I was wearing an Augmented hooded sweatshirt.

The Middle Eastern owner gave us the look he always gives us. Since we all keep our hair really short and basically all dress the same, I suppose to him we either look like a gang or a bunch of neo-Nazis. We must've been in this 7-11 a million times and we've probably bought at least that many Slurpees off him, but none of that seems to matter. He always looks at us with caution.

I put a little bit of ice in my Big Gulp cup and started filling it with Coke. Everyone says that caffeine keeps you awake but it has absolutely no effect on me. Adam walked over to the Slurpee machine and started to fill his cup with blue Slurpee.

"How can you drink that stuff?" I laughed.

"Dude," he smiled, "it's sooooo good."

"It's too much sugar for right now."

"Should I get a bean burrito or nachos?" Carlo asked looking at both choices in the bin by the counter.

"Neither," I start, "you'll throw up if you eat that stuff this late."

The door to the 7-11 jingled open and some rap music was faintly heard coming from a car that just pulled up. People say it a lot about hardcore music, but all that deep, bass music with people singing about their cars, girls and money all sounds the same to me. At least hardcore tries to sing about issues that matter to people like the environment, corruption in the government, and the dangers of drug and alcohol abuse.

A stocky, Mexican kid walked in with a tall guy behind him. The tall guy stayed in the front area of the store while the stocky Mexican came over by us. I moved past him as he went to the Big Gulp machine. He took one extra large Big Gulp cup and filled it with Dr. Pepper and then he took another cup and filled it with ice. Adam started to walk over to me as the Mexican guy glided past him holding both cups.

"Excuse me," Adam says but the Mexican guy doesn't even acknowledge him on the way to the counter.

"Should I get some candy?" I asked, eyeing the row of sweets in front of us.

"You can," Adam starts. "I'm cool with this Blue Slurpee."

"I just want a tiny piece of candy, nothing too big or..."

"ONE'S FILLED WITH COKE AND THE OTHER'S FILLED WITH ICE!!!!!" the Mexican guy suddenly yelled at the Middle Eastern man behind the counter.

Right away, I know what the problem is.

At 7-11 if you buy a drink and then take an extra cup, you get charged the same amount for the extra cup as you do for the drink. It doesn't matter if there's nothing in it. I found out these rules in a different way when Augmented first had stickers made up. I saved a Slurpee cup and put a sticker on it. Then I brought the old cup to that 7-11 (this was right before all the 7-11s started allowing customers to self-serve their own Slurpees) and the Middle Eastern man behind the counter refused to fill it. I thought he was just kidding but then he tersely informed me of the rules. It was an old cup and because of health codes he couldn't fill it up again. He then also told me about the extra cup rule.

"I'm sorry. You took two cups I have to charge you for two." The Middle Eastern man said to the Mexican guy.

"IT'S JUST A CUP WITH ICE!!!"

"THAT'S THE POLICY!! IF YOU TAKE ANOTHER CUP YOU WILL BE CHARGED FOR TWO!!"

"I'M ONLY BUYING ONE THING!!"

"I HAVE TO CHARGE YOU FOR TWO!! IT'S STORE INVENTORY! NOW EITHER YOU PAY OR YOU GET OUT!!"

"THIS ISN'T EVEN YOUR COUNTRY!!! YOU CAN'T TELL ME WHAT TO DO!!! WHY ARE YOU EVEN HERE?!?!?"

"IT'S MY STORE!! WHAT DO I DO HERE?!? WHERE'S MY COUNTRY?!?! WHERE'S YOUR COUNTRY?!?!"

The Mexican guy and his friend started to walk out of the 7-11 leaving the cups on the counter. I wondered if they were going to get some of their friends out of the car which was still running.

"GO BACK TO YOUR OWN COUNTRY!!! YOU CAMEL JOCKEY!!!"

The two Mexican guys were out the door and the Middle Eastern owner started following after them. I guess telling someone to "go back to their own country" really pisses them off, because I had never seen the Middle Eastern man come to the other side of the counter before. He opened the door to the 7-11 so he could continue yelling at the Mexican guy.

"GO BACK TO MY COUNTRY?!?! WHERE IS MY COUNTRY?!?! GO BACK WHERE?!?! WHERE AM I FROM?!?!"

Any minute now I was expecting a car full of Mexican guys to jump out and beat up the Middle Eastern man, but they just yelled a few choice words back at him and drove away. Once the Middle Eastern man was sure they were gone, he came back into the 7-11 and went behind the counter again.

Chapter 4

I didn't wake up the next morning until almost 11:30 am. I get pretty wired before and after our shows, so that by the time I eventually do go to bed, I'm beat. I didn't get home until about 2 am, and I didn't really start sleeping until 3 am. So I guess all things considered, waking up at almost noon isn't that bad.

I didn't get up right away. I just laid in bed, feeling good for no reason other then I was happy with my band, my girlfriend, school... my life. I looked over at the poster Isaac made for us when he released our first 7". It's a shot of us playing in front of about twenty five people. The way Shayna took the picture she made it look like a lot more. Isaac had made up a bunch of posters and my dad tried to hide his surprise when I first showed them to him. My folks support what I do but to them the music I play just sounds like noise. I'm willing to bet that the music they liked just sounded like noise to their parents, too. I like the music my parents listened to like Led Zeppelin, The Rolling Stones and The Who. Sometimes when I listen to those groups I can't believe that my parents ever liked that stuff. My mom has always seemed more open minded about my music than my dad. Don't get me wrong, I think he's happy that his son is interested in something, I just think he thinks I put too much time into it.

Next to the Augmented poster were a few pictures of Erika and I. There was one of us from the first Christmas we were together, another from when we took a road trip to Santa Barbara (it was for an Augmented show) and a few others. Sometimes I'll stare at a picture of us and I'll remember that before that picture was taken we had made out, argued, had sex, etc. Because of that, I can't look at pictures of people now without wondering what was happening to them before the picture was taken. It seems like when all you see is a part of something you can never get the whole story.

I got out of bed and made my way downstairs. My house is pretty big. It probably seems that way because there's only 3 people living in it. I'm an only child but I've never minded it. It's just how it was and that was that.

My dad is an architect and works from home. He owns his own business called Interior Installations. He works up in Los Angeles a lot and only sometimes in Orange County. I don't think he likes to drive to L.A. but he does it. My mom works at a bank close to our house. I wouldn't say that we're rich, just middle-class. Maybe upper-middle class but definitely not rich.

I went to the pantry and took out a box of Fruity Pebbles, a bowl and a spoon. On the way to the table I grabbed the milk out of the refrigerator. I like Fruity Pebbles with very little milk. I find that I get a good mix of soggy and hard pebbles and that's when it tastes best. I started to look at the newspaper which my mom left on the table; she always does that. We get two papers sent to the house and she's the only one who really reads any of them, and even she usually never gets past the first couple of articles in the Local section.

My dad walked into the room wearing a suit and carrying a briefcase, so chances are he was headed up to Los Angeles. Seeing as how it's summertime, I sorta feel bad for him. Lately, I've been catching myself looking at my dad and wondering if I look like him, or, when I get a little older, if I'm going to look like him. I do this now and he catches me.

"Where are you going?" I asked, even though I already knew the answer.

"L.A." He says indifferently. When my dad gives quick answers that is a sure sign that he doesn't want to talk about something.

"In this heat?"

My dad shot me another look and then picked up a 9x12 manila envelope. It's orientation papers from Purdue University. I'm supposed to be starting school there in the fall. I haven't mentioned it much and I hadn't been thinking about it much, even though the time is fast approaching when I'm supposed to be leaving. It seems like it's really far away and I can continue to put it off... even though I know I can't.

"This came for you."

"I know," I said taking the envelope. I put it on top of the newspaper.

"Are you working today?"

"Yeah, at 3."

"Are you gonna be home for supper?"

"No, I'm eating out with Erika."

"Well," he said gathering up his things. "I'll see you later. If mom calls tell her she can reach me on my cellphone."

"Okay."

I put some Fruity Pebbles in my mouth. I looked down at the orientation papers and decided that going away to school was still too far way to really think about. I turned my attention back to the newspaper. On page three there was a headline that said:

THE FUTURE HAS A NEW FACE

Under that was a picture of a bunch of Asian and Mexican kids smiling. I stared at the picture for a moment. "These kids would be cute if they weren't Asian or Mexican," I jokingly thought to myself. Then I turned the page of the newspaper, forgetting I ever had that thought.

Chapter 5

I love listening to music when I drive to work. For the past three weeks I'd been listening to nothing but the new Corruption CD. They're an older, straight edge band from New York. They used to be good friends with Benji Walker but they had a falling out for some reason. Their CD wasn't even out yet but Isaac had given Carlo a copy with the explicit warning not to make any copies for anyone else. Well, of course Carlo made copies for Russ and I, and then Adam wanted one... so you can see how well not making copies went. It was such a good record. It wasn't that fast but it wasn't slow. You wouldn't really "pit" to it, you'd sort of just move in place with everybody else (which in my opinion are the best kind of pits). Truthfully, Corruption's CD was inspiring me to write different types of songs for Augmented.

As I drove I noticed that O'Neils, a barbecue restaurant I had been going to my whole life, was going out of business. Out in front of it were some Asian people and they had placed a cheap, plastic, yellow banner over the O'Neils' sign. The restaurant was now going to be called Pho something or other. I'd seen names like that before but I can never pronounce them. I wondered how many people in this area would eat at a place like that, but I then remembered that in areas like Garden Grove these places were more prevalent. Garden Grove was just north of Fountain Valley. I guess my city was getting some spillover. That had actually been the subject of the newspaper article I had seen that morning. At least I think that was the subject, I didn't really read the article.

Chapter 6

"Come on, Mike! You're going too slow!!" I said with mock seriousness.

"Us Asians like to take it slow, we like to go with the flow," Mike stated casually.

Baha Burgers was going off today. We usually did good business for lunch but it was almost five o'clock and it hadn't stopped since my shift started at 3. Working summers was the best because the restaurant was located right on the beach in Huntington. The girls would come in wearing bikinis and looking insanely hot. There were plenty of hot girls in HB (the short name for Huntington Beach) but summer seemed to bring them all out, and it was like they all came to Baha Burgers.

I usually worked with Mike Nguyen. He had moved to Huntington Beach from Santa Ana about three months ago. His parents lived in Garden Grove. Baha Burgers also employed these Mexican cooks named Jesus and Ramiro. They didn't speak English that well but they taught us words in Spanish. Bad words. I loved working there and a few months ago I was offered a full-time, management-type job, but with the band, school and knowing I was probably going away to Indiana, I didn't take it.

"You're number 9," I said to a young skater kid and his friend as I handed them back their change and receipt.

"Yeah, he is," one of his friends smiled. "He's a real nine." They both laughed and walked away from the counter. Man, I remember when I was their age. Being in elementary school, summer would come and you'd have three months off to do whatever you wanted. The thought of those times ending never entered your mind and then when they do end you don't even realize it.

"Too bad your slowness is costing the company money," I smiled. Mike looked at me because he'd forgotten I was still insulting him. "I'm gonna have to tell the boss to take it out of your paycheck."

"Paycheck, chhhhh...." Mike smiled, taking a slight rest from the constant influx of customers. It seemed like we'd handled the rush for now. "I'll bet if they put a blindfold on me I'd still move faster then you, fool. You just get the easy orders."

"Mike... they wouldn't need a blindfold to cover your eyes."

I laughed and turned as Mike punched me in shoulder. This was par for the course. We must punch each other at least 50 times during a shift.

"Man, whiteboy, I'm gonna mess you up!"

He tried to hit me again but I blocked the punch.

Chapter 7

Looking back at everything, I shouldn't have been surprised with the way things went. Especially with my band. The thing that was sadly the most important thing to me in the world. I only say "sadly" because the band was more important to me then certain people in my life. For awhile there, I was also clueless to some of the things happening in my band. I was so naive thinking I could continue to juggle everything that I didn't realize certain feelings that people like Carlo and Russ had about me. Carlo resented the fact that as much as I cared about the band, it always seemed to mean more to him than it did to me. I wasn't able to do the one thing the guys wanted to do most in the world. The thing that might've made all the difference for our band.

Touring.

Not being able to be everywhere at once, I knew that Carlo wasn't keeping his mouth shut about not being happy with me (even though he hadn't said anything to my face). He always acted like everything was "cool." Knowing that Russ was always there for some good smack talking sessions, I'm sure it became easier and easier to see me as an impediment to Augmented's progress. Anyway, I had people like Isaac and Adam fill me in on most of the details once the summer was over. After this summer I would have a lot of time to think and that helped me piece everything together so that I could have it all make sense. All that thinking made me realize just how confused I'd been.

Carlo would have done anything for Augmented. That's the one thing that really drove us together and it seemed to become the only thing we talked about. That was another thing I didn't realize until later.

He would hang out with Isaac at the Pushing Forth Records Warehouse for hours trying to set stuff up. Then he would call all of us to let us know what he and Isaac had talked about. It eventually seemed like nothing Carlo did was selflessly motivated. It was all in the name of promoting the band. I think that all started the day Isaac called Carlo after he listened to our first demo and said he wanted to put our record out.

"I'm telling you Carlo, you guys should go out this summer. At least for a week, just tour the West Coast."

Isaac and Carlo had gone to Blueprint Records. This was a local record store in Huntington Beach that sold almost exclusively old and new punk and hardcore music. It was really small but it was packed with 12" and 7" records, as well as CDs by bands that, unless you were somehow involved in one of the music scenes (punk, hardcore, emo, etc.), you probably had never heard of them. It was also a hangout. I didn't go there a lot but when I did I could always count on somebody being there, either shopping in the store or working behind the counter, that I knew from going to shows.

"I want to," Carlo began, "it's Tim. He can't because he has to work."

"He can't take a week off?" Isaac asked. "Other than road trips to San Diego and Arizona, where else have you guys played other than here?"

"We haven't, I know." Carlo stammered.

Isaac absentmindedly checked the 7" bin to make sure that Pushing Forth Records were well represented. He eyed Carlo.

"Look Carlo, it's not like you guys are going to get any bigger. How do you think Corruption sold 25,000 records? They toured all the time. Playing the same places over and over again. That's with no radio help, no video support on MTV... nothing. Just touring. That's why they're able to not work and just do the band full time. The thing is they have to keep touring and writing records otherwise they can't survive."

Isaac stared at Carlo to make sure he understood this. Carlo did. Without touring, without really going for it, Augmented would never be anything more than it was now. A big band in a local scene.

"Can't you get somebody to fill in for Tim?"

"He'd be bummed." Carlo stated.

They continued to move around the store. Carlo wasn't getting the answers he wanted and Isaac was half in the conversation and half thinking about how he could sell more records. Isaac was always thinking like that and that's probably why he'd been so successful.

"Well, then tell Tim to sack up and take a week off work."

"He can't. He's going away to school. He says he needs to save up money."

"Aren't his parents helping him out?"

"Yeah," Carlo exclaimed. "He doesn't even need to work but he does. He could just focus on the band if he really wanted to, but I think he's scared of what his parents would say."

"That's really punk rock." Isaac smiled sarcastically.

"Yeah, I know."

"What are you guys gonna do when he leaves?"

"Play when he comes home, I guess." Carlo now realized he wasn't giving Isaac the answers he wanted. "The holidays. He's home for like three months in the summer."

Isaac turned to Carlo and gave him his full attention.

"No offense, Carlo, I mean, Tim's a good guy, but your band isn't going to get any bigger playing like that. You gotta commit yourself to it. Otherwise you'll just get so big, then one day you won't be that big anymore. There'll be another band, younger than you guys... and they'll be more dialed into the scene; just like you guys are now. Trust me, I've seen it happen. What about the other guys in Augmented? How do they feel?"

"They're into it. We all are. They just want to play. Russ wants to go to Europe and Adam, he's just stoked to be in this band. They want to do everything."

Chapter 8

Practice.

I loved practicing. I could seriously do it for 8 to 10 hours a day. Sometimes we practiced at Adam's and other times at Russ's parents house. He and Carlo moved in together a few months ago. We tried to practice in the garage that they had at their apartment but it was too loud and small. We agreed we'd only practice there again if it was an emergency.

Adam's parents were cool and they let us put Augmented posters all over their garage. They even bought us a dry erase board so we could write our set list's on them. It didn't take long for Carlo and Russ to draw X rated pictures on it. I don't even want to go into what they were, just know that as soon as they left, Adam erased the drawings before his parents saw them. I think Adam's folks know that we're all generally good guys. I also think that when they see that their kid has an interest in something, especially when he's 16 like Adam, they're probably just happy that it isn't drugs or alcohol. I wonder if they even knew we were a straight edge band? He said they were really impressed with our CD. Not the music of course, they couldn't actually listen to it, but just the fact that all that noise from their garage had actually produced something tangible. That somebody else had put their time and money into their son's band.

We always tried to play our set three times. The key for us was to get into a rhythm so that all the songs seamlessly blended into one another like I said before. My goal would be that we'd never stop playing. Our set would seem really short, like one big song, but it would actually be like 10 or 13 songs. This way we would leave people wanting more. Sometimes I wondered where I had learned this stuff. How to perform? Leaving them wanting more? Ask any of us and we wouldn't know, because for a hardcore band it isn't about performance as much as it is the need to communicate something to someone else. At least that's what I like to think it is... but sometimes it does feel like we're performing. Or we have to perform.

Adam's parents also bought us a small refrigerator that we kept stocked with juice and water. After practice we usually stuck around for about a half hour and talked about the band. Not about the music really, just about the band. Where are we going? What are we doing? That kind of thing. Sometimes, though it was rare, we'd even start practicing again.

"So, Barwill tells me that the Mexicans that live next door to him always have these parties that go on forever. And they're always really loud. So a few nights ago, he called the cops." Russ was talking about this guy we all knew named John Barwill. His parents had moved to Arizona and he and his sister were taking care of their house. Apparently, they'd been having some problems with their neighbors.

"How late was it?" Carlo asked.

"I think it was like 12. So the police come, the party ends, and around 2 am John and his sister are finally getting to sleep when there's a knock on the door."

"No way!" I couldn't help spit out. Now this story was really getting interesting.

"Yeah, and it's the Mexican kid's Mom!"

"Was she apologizing for them?" Adam asked.

"No! She's pissed at John and his sister for calling the cops!"

"Two hours later she came over?!?!" Carlo was almost in a state of disbelief.

"Yeah. So she starts yelling at John and he's like, 'Don't you have any respect?' So eventually, she leaves. He says things have been cool since, but dude, to even have to deal with that."

"They'll probably have another party soon for one of the other 8 million members of their family." Carlo laughed.

"I was reading in the newspaper that by about 2025 the majority of people in O.C. are either going to be Mexican or Asian," I stated. I wasn't trying to sound racist or anything but I'm sure that's how I sounded.

"That sucks," Carlo said. "What about us?"

"Then he was telling me," Russ started again, "that they have this piece of shit, yellow truck. It hasn't worked in over 10 months and they just leave it broken down on their front lawn. Dude, how ghetto is that?"

I laughed. We all did. I guess White people just do things differently. Some Asians who live in my tract park their cars on their front lawns from time to time. I sometimes want to ask them if the street was really that crowded.

"I went to Blueprint with Isaac on Tuesday," Carlo said changing the subject.

"What'd he say?" I asked.

"Yeah, is he gonna buy us a van?"

"He would," Carlo said slowly, "if we we were gonna tour."

"We are aren't we?" Adam got himself a drink from the fridge.

"I can't," I started, not really looking anybody in the eye because even I didn't think my reason was a good excuse. "I don't have the money. I'm trying to work now so that I'll be able to help my parents out with school."

"He was just saying that we could get a lot bigger if we toured. He says our records sell really well on the West Coast, and they also sell well on the East Coast and in places like Chicago, too. We also sell a lot in Europe. He was saying we should tour the states, then maybe tour Europe with Corruption in late Fall or Spring. He says we can probably even go out with them for a week on the East Coast in August if we want to."

"That would be rad!!" Russ said, very excited.

"Yeah," Adam chimed in.

"Come on, Tim!!! Blow off school!!" Carlo joked.

"I'd like to," I said, again not really looking at any of them. "But I can't. It's just... I can't."

"Yeah," Carlo offered. He was still smiling.

Nobody said anything. For a second, it was as though we were waiting for someone who wasn't in the room to say something. To make things not be so awkward. Adam absent-mindedly hit his snare drum a few times.

"Lets run through the last five songs of the set." Carlo finally said.

"Okay." I got in my stance to start playing again. I started to imagine what it would be like in Europe. Playing to a packed crowd. Opening for Corruption. It would be great and I knew it.

Chapter 9

Erika and I were driving to the mall in her car. Before her, I had never had a girlfriend this awesome. It wasn't just her looks, in other ways I thought she was perfect. I think she knew I felt this way, but she was so cool (in a good way), so self-assured, she never had to really ask me what I thought of her. She had a way of dressing that was almost effortless in its sense of style. She didn't dress like any of the other girls. Whereas Carlo and Russ went out with punk chicks, and Adam was with a typical California blonde, Erika wasn't any of those things. She stood out in the way I think a girl wants to stand out. Sometimes I wondered what she was doing with me. I mostly wear jeans and t-shirts. I don't dress like a slob or anything but I don't really put much thought into what I wear. When I buy new clothes, I always take Erika with me just because I know she has a better sense of style than I do.

"So are you definitely going away to school?" Erika asked. She was the only person I had told that I was having doubts. I think she was a lot happier about my having doubts than she was letting on.

"It looks that way," I said somewhat uneasily. Around her, I didn't have to hide how I felt so much. I was sort of bummed that she had brought this up, only because we were having such a good time talking and laughing. It was just a downer of a subject. "I started looking at the orientation paperwork. They have a thing they set up called a Boiler Gold Rush where you go out there for like five days. You stay on campus before school starts and basically pretend you're a student."

"Can I come?" She asked jokingly.

Cool, this meant the conversation wouldn't get too serious. I was doing a pretty good job of not thinking about any of this stuff. Now, if only I could avoid my Dad more.

"I wish." I smiled.

"You know I'm getting my own apartment when I transfer to UCLA, right?"

"I'll probably do that. Maybe next year. I wish we were going to school together." And I did, too, not just because we'd have our own places and we could always stay over and everything. I wished we could ALWAYS be together, but I didn't want to say that right now. That was a line I was saving in case the conversation got too serious about me leaving.

"Me too," she started. I was starting to think this conversation was going to get a bit heavy. I just wanted to relax, hang out, go to the mall, eat, and then go somewhere and hookup a little bit. "But we've already been over this. You don't want to live in L.A. and I'm not ready to move to Indiana."

"I guess we'll have to make the most out of the holidays and the summer." I could've told her if she really loved me she'd come with me to Indiana, but that would've been stupid. She did love me and I knew it.

"But you'll be playing with the band then."

This conversation was reaching a point where I had to start thinking of other stuff for us talk about. We were taking a wrong turn and if I didn't get it back in the right direction, the conversation would start going all over the place and I'd say something wrong, she'd nail me on it and then the day would be ruined. This rarely happened, and I know in relationships it needs to happen, but that didn't mean that I had to walk around trying to make it happen.

"Yeah, but once I start school," I started, choosing my words very carefully even though I wanted it to seem like I wasn't. "I won't have to work, so I won't be working on the holidays when I come home. I might not even work during the summer."

"You'll just be doing the band full time." She wasn't trying to start an argument. She never tried to do that. I probably had done things to make her feel insecure or something, and while she had kept pretty cool about it, I could tell that the things she was saying weren't just being made up on the spot. She had done some thinking about all of this stuff. "You'll go on tour and then you'll never be around."

I laughed a little bit. I couldn't help it. She stared at me slightly and I gave her an over dramatic frown.

"I'm being serious."

She laughed a little bit after she said that. Neither of us said anything for a few moments. I looked out the window at some Asian and Mexican restaurants that had been there for about two years. It didn't seem like they'd ever been here until now. There was another banner over a sign where a frame shop had been. It was going to be a $1 Dollar Store now.

"There's a lot more Asian places here now." I said, still staring out the window. I was comforted for a moment by the site of shops and restaurants I had gone to when I was a kid that were still there.

"Yeah," Erika said. She looked out the window a little bit too. I looked at her face. At her tan skin and soft cheek structure. I felt bad. I hadn't meant that comment to end the talk we were having, like I didn't care about her feelings. She knew I did. However, if we could start talking about something else that was fine by me.

"It's weird, places that I've seen all my life have changed right under my nose. Like that Asian place. I was used to it being Luparello's Pizza. Now it's Hung Dhuc something or other."

"That place has been here for like four years." Erika laughed.

"I know, I just never noticed it before." I looked out the window again. "Look at that place, it used to be George's Burgers, now it's a Pizza and Mediterranean Chicken Restaurant. What happened to everything? Why am I just noticing it now?"

"Because you're a racist."

Erika smiled at me. Now this was starting to become a good conversation again. The kind where two people do nothing but lob insults that show how much they like each other.

"Yeah, I'm really a racist having a Mexican girlfriend."

"What about that place?"

She pointed out the window. I had to sit up a bit so I could see it. I've always thought she drives too fast. I missed it.

"Cantamar Mexican Restaurant?"

"What about it?" I smiled. "It's a beaner joint."

She laughed. She knew I didn't mean it.

"What does Cantamar mean?"

"I don't know. That it's good?" I laughed a little, half wondering why on earth she would think I'd know what "Cantamar" meant.

"I doubt it."

"So what does it mean my hot, latina, brown-power friend?"

"I don't know?"

We both laughed. Today was going to be a good day after all.

I loved going to the mall during the week. It's not as crowded, plus, it's like a place suspended in time from my childhood. No matter which mall I go to, as long as it's during the day, that's how it feels for some reason. I used to go to Westminster Mall a lot with Carlo in the summer. We'd take the bus, hang out all day and then take the bus home. Sometimes we'd just ride the bus all day. That's how come when I started driving I knew where everything was. At the mall we'd go to the movies all day or steal food from the stores that offered free samples. Then we stopped doing that for some reason. In fact, it wasn't until we started doing Augmented that we really started hanging out a lot again.

Erika and I had gone into a record store and to my surprise that was where I saw it. The Augmented CD. It was in the same CD bin, in the same store, with all the other bands in the world. The Augmented All the Way Back CD was available everywhere.

"Man, Isaac moves fast. Carlo says our records are everywhere."

"Should I buy it?" Erika asked.

I gave her a funny look. She had it before it came out. I made her a copy as soon as I had one.

"I gave you one. In fact, I think I gave you more than one."

"So? I wanna show you that I support your band."

"I know you do. I support you too, don't I?"

"Yeah."

"So why are you complaining?" I smiled.

I walked out of the record store knowing that Erika would follow me. I was waiting for her to come up next to me when I felt her hands on my shoulders. I stopped as she hoisted herself up so I could give her a piggyback ride. Nobody really stared at us as we walked around the mall like a couple of 10-year-olds.

We passed by a clothing store. It was the kind where all the sales girls could be models, and only the really hot girls shop there because the clothing line doesn't cater to any other type of person.

"Lets go in there." She asked.

I kept walking. I was hungry and I knew a stop in there would take at least 20-30 minutes.

"Tim!" Erika wrapped her arms around my neck as if she was going to strangle me. I loved the way her skin felt.

"Come on, lets get something to eat?"

"But I want to go into that store!?!"

"I'm hungry," I whined back.

"Fine," Erika said as she relaxed her grip around my neck. "We won't go in that store, Mr. 'I Support My Girlfriend'."

We passed by some cholo guys and their chola girlfriends. You don't run into too much of that at South Coast Plaza or the Crystal Court in Costa Mesa, but we had gone to Westminster Mall today and the area was different.

I loved the look the chola's had. Big hair, lots of make-up, but dressed down. The guys had a look that wasn't much different than mine. Their clothes were baggier, but they all had pretty short haircuts, they wore sneakers, etc. The main difference was that they looked tougher then I ever could. Sure, a bunch of straight edge guys might look tough in a group with our hooded sweatshirts and shaved heads, but for a cholo guy in just a simple white t-shirt and khaki pants, he looked tough whether there was one or 100 of them. The cholos looked passed me and focused on Erika, speaking amongst themselves in Spanish.

"Yeah, Erika, being checked out by the homies," I said when I thought we were far enough away.

"How do you know that they were checking me out?" she asked coyly.

"I don't think they were looking at me. Plus, I know Spanish."

"You do not."

"Certain words. I'm probably more Mexican than you are."

"You mean Latino."

"Whatever." I looked around the mall some. "Where do you want to eat?

We walked out of the parking lot holding hands and carrying our bags. We passed by the same group of Mexican people we had seen about an hour earlier inside the mall. They stood next to a lowered truck, with tinted windows and oversized hubcaps. They were listening to some loud hip-hop music. I always wondered how people drove around listening to that type of music at such loud levels, but then if they heard the music I listen to at similar volumes, they'd probably wonder the same thing. Some of the Mexican guys made comments, this time in English, about Erika. They weren't bad, at least I didn't think they were bad. I think guys are happy when other guys are envious of their girlfriend. Erika looked at me like she thought they were dorks and I smiled.

I probably smiled a little bit too much because that's when one of the cholos got in my face. He was a little shorter than me but he was stocky. He had a few tattoos on the lower parts of his arms and a small one on his neck. With or without his friends, this guy could kill me.

"You think something's funny, eh?" He was inches from my face. I went cold inside. His breath didn't smell as bad as I thought it would.

"No."

I was so scared. Erika was pulling my hand to keep me walking. I didn't realize how hard she was pulling until we talked later.

"Why are you smiling then? You were smiling earlier when we saw you also." I didn't know what was scaring me more, that he was in my face or that he was so calm about it.

"Leave them alone." One of the chola girls said to him.

"Stop being a jerk, Oscar!" One of his friends offered.

I half wanted to thank them.

"It's still a free country, right?" I asked with a glare. I had no idea why I was being brave. Erika and I were free to walk away.

"You wanna start something?" His eyes were angry. I stared deep into them and realized that this guy hated me. He didn't even know me and he hated me. And I hated him right back.

"I'm a little outnumbered, aren't I?"

"Why don't you leave us alone? We weren't bothering you?" Erika sounded cute, especially when she was mad. Oscar looked at Erika, surprised.

"Your girl's got a big mouth, man." He moved closer to me. I let go of Erika's hand and could feel her getting scared. It was looking more and more like I was a dead man. Why did I care what this guy thought? Erika would be happier if I didn't fight. Win or lose, she hated that stuff. I used to say she was the only Mexican alive that didn't like boxing.

"Look," I started, "we were just walking. I thought of something funny and I smiled about it, that's all. It had nothing to do with you."

"It better not," He replied.

We continued to stare at each other for a few moments longer until Erika grabbed my hand again and we walked away.

Chapter 10

Carlo and Russ were shooting around on a basketball court at a park that was near their apartment. None of us really played basketball but it was still fun to shoot baskets from time to time.

"So who else can we get?" Carlo asked after he missed a free throw. Russ grabbed the ball and bounced it a bit as he walked to the free throw line. Carlo stood under the basket.

"What about Benji?"

"Yeah," Carlo started, "but he's not that good." He'd already thought of Benji Walker to fill in for me when I went away, because he was a little older then all of us and he was more "hardcore" in terms of how he lived. He was covered in tattoos, he drank a lot. It had even been rumored that he had done, and still did, cocaine and heroin. Benji had been to jail for assault but he claimed it wasn't his fault. He also had a lot of friends in the hardcore scene.

"How good does he have to be for a one week tour?" Russ threw up the ball and it swooshed through the net. Carlo threw it back to him.

"Yeah, but dude... you don't want people to see us for the first time and think we suck."

"Yeah," Russ began, "then they'd think we did everything in the studio."

"Dude, I can't believe Tim won't take off work for one week and do a tour. It's not like the money he's making at his job is even gonna matter for school. His parents are footing the bill. When does he think we're ever going to get this chance again?"

Russ and Carlo hadn't noticed a white, lowered Honda with a long fin (most people called them spoilers) on the back, pull up. Two Asian guys got out of the car. One of them carried a basketball. Russ saw them when they got a little closer.

"Check out that shopping cart, dude. What do you wanna do?"

The Asian guys had come here to play basketball and chances are they would want to play with them. Or at least share the court.

"Screw 'em," Carlo said. "We were here first." He took the ball from Russ and shot it.

"You know there's gonna be more coming. Gooks always travel in packs."

The two Asian guys walked on to the court.

"You guys want to play two on two?" One of them asked.

Carlo didn't even look at them. "Nope." Russ said nonchalantly.

The two Asian guys used the other half of the court.

"They think they own this place," Carlo said in a low tone.

"In few years, they probably will," Russ laughed.

A few minutes later another lowered car pulled up. Its windows were tinted. Behind it was another car that hadn't had any work done to it. Six Asians got out of one car and five got out of the other. They had basketballs as well.

"Jesus, look how many they fit in each car," Russ laughed. Carlo smiled. The other Asian guy that was already there came over to them. The one they hadn't spoken with yet.

"Hey, why don't you guys play with us so we can use the whole court?" he asked.

Russ and Carlo didn't even look at him. Carlo threw the ball up, missed again, and Russ went and got it.

"You guys have a problem?"

"Yeah." Russ said as he turned to face him. "We have a real big problem."

"Solve it then." The Asian guy offered.

"Nah, not today, but we will," Carlo grinned.

He walked off the court and Russ followed after him. When they got a little further away, they both cracked up laughing.

Chapter 11

Today we practiced at Russ's parents house. We were all set up and ready to go except for Adam. He always took the longest out of any of us. In fact, he was still bringing in his cymbals from the car. I took this time to tell Russ and Carlo about my run in with the cholo at the mall.

"Mexicans don't believe in a fair fight," Russ stated flatly.

"You mess with one bean, you get the whole burrito," Carlo smiled.

"It was like those nips the other night. They actually thought we were gonna fight them. The two of us Carlo, versus all the slopes they could squeeze into a Mitsubishi."

"At least like the Italian and Irish mobs have class." Carlo started. "Even the Black gangs have more class then the Mexican and Asian mafias. Those people don't even respect themselves, like that stuff Barwill was telling you about his neighbors being loud."

"They probably shouldn't even be in this country." Russ offered.

"That's mighty White of you, Russ," I smiled as I tuned up my guitar a little bit.

"And what's wrong with that?" He asked seriously.

I had to laugh. So did Carlo. I didn't agree with Russ but I don't think I entirely disagreed either.

"Oh yeah," Carlo began, "Isaac got us a show at the Macondo."

"Really?" I asked.

"No way!" Adam exclaimed.

"Yeah, we're opening but who cares... it's in Hollywood, right?"

"Who are we playing with?" Russ asked.

"He said the lineup wasn't confirmed, but it'll probably be with two L.A. bands. Function might come down from Seattle."

"That's rad, man. Isaac rules." Russ seemed to forgot the other stuff he'd been saying. He started playing some notes on his bass.

"Have any of you guys seen my ride stand?" Adam asked.

"No," I replied.

"Why would we have seen it?" Russ asked impatiently. Adam could really lag sometimes.

"I don't know, but I can't find it. I guess I can play without it today."

"You think you left it at home?" Carlo asked.

"No, I wouldn't have."

"Go out and look in your car again." Russ was starting to get pissed. Stuff like this always seemed to bother him more than Carlo and I.

"That's what I've been doing." Adam was starting to get mad too. Russ was always on him. Adam would put up with it for a while but eventually he'd start to fight back.

"You think someone may have stolen it?" Carlo asked into the microphone so his voice was amplified over the PA system. "While you were bringing your stuff in?"

"I don't think so."

"But," I began, "you did set up a lot of your kit while you were loading in. Did you leave the back door of your car open?"

"I'll bet those kids outside took it," Russ offered. There had been some kids playing a few houses over across the street.

"No."

"Why not, Adam? They see a car full of stuff they think it's theirs. They don't care."

"Lets go out and look in your car." We all followed Carlo out of the garage.

"He probably left it at home." Carlo had looked all around Adam's car. I briefly wondered if Adam minded that just because he was 3-4 years younger than us, we always treated him like he was a lot younger. I tried not to do it too much just because I know from personal experience with my father that it sucks to have someone second guess you all the time.

"Maybe I did, but I doubt it."

"Screw it, just play without it. Let's practice." I had to be at work at 3 and we'd already blown about a half hour of practice. I started to walk back into the garage.

"Those kids, I told you!" Russ said angrily.

I turned back around.

"What are you talking about?" Carlo asked.

"There's two kids watching us and hiding. White trash, ghetto..." Russ started mumbling as he walked towards them. I looked a bit in the distance and saw who Russ was referring to. There were two kids, one was White and the other was Mexican, watching us a few houses down in a garage across the street. When they saw that we had seen them they hid back inside the garage.

"Where are you going?" I yelled after him.

"To get the stand back!!"

Carlo and I looked at each other.

"He's such an idiot, dude." Carlo said shaking his head.

Russ walked up to the one story house where the garage was open. For some reason, the kids walked out onto the driveway almost as if to meet him. They stopped walking when Russ started yelling at them. He was yelling so loud I could hear him perfectly from where I was standing. After a few moments, an older guy came out of the house and pushed Russ. This guy I knew because he and his friends hung around in my neighborhood. His name was Bradley. I generally knew who he was but I'd never actually met him. I sort of always made it a point to stay away from him and his friends. All they seemed to do was hang around the park by my house, smoke cigarettes and hide the beer that they were drinking if a cop came by. I had even heard that they sold drugs out of the park, too.

"Great!" Carlo said as he started running over to Russ. Adam and I followed behind him. It was amazing to me how not three minutes earlier we were about to practice.

Now, we might be having a fight over a missing cymbal stand.

"Don't be messing with my brother! I'll kick your ass!!" Bradley yelled. He pushed Russ as we all came up behind him. Our presence didn't deter Bradley at all. "Oh what's this? You guys wanna go?"

"Do you?" Carlo asked calmly. I could never have been that calm. I hate fighting. Even around those Mexican guys at the mall, I don't think I sounded as calm as I'd wanted to.

"Not with four guys but if you wanna roll, we'll roll!"

"Ask them if they took my stand." Adam asked.

We looked at the two kids. I assumed the White one was Bradley's brother.

"Did you take it?!?!" Russ yelled.

"Don't yell at my brother!! I'll kill you!!!" Bradley was just as pissed at Russ which seemed to do nothing but make Russ more angry.

"Try it! I'm not scared of you, Bradley!!"

Russ pushed Bradley. I grabbed Russ, which I figured was safer, and Carlo got in front of Bradley.

"What are you doing, dude?!?!" I asked Russ. He didn't hear me. You never hear people when you're really angry about something.

"Relax," Carlo said to Bradley.

"Screw all you guys! I'll reek on each one of you!!" Bradley pushed Carlo now.

"Whoa," Carlo said as he got his balance. He stared at Bradley for a moment. "Just ask them if they took it. Then we'll leave."

"Screw this guy, Carlo!! I'll beat his ass back to the trailer park!!" Russ yelled.

"Your mom's in my trailer park!" Bradley punctuated that response by giving Russ the finger.

"Did you guys take it?" Carlo asked the two kids. They were too scared to answer and I couldn't blame them. "DID YOU TAKE IT?"

"No," the White kid said in a low tone. The Mexican kid looked at Carlo and slowly nodded his head. The White kid saw him. "I did not Javier!!"

"You did too, Randy!!" Javier seemed like he was getting mad now.

"Look, just give it back." I said.

"Yeah," Adam chimed in, "it's mine."

Bradley turned to Randy. "Did you take it?"

"No."

Bradley socked his brother in the arm.

"DON'T LIE!!!"

"I DIDN'T TAKE IT!!" Randy yelled. He ran into the house crying. Javier looked really scared now as Bradley turned to him.

"Where is it?!?" He sounded just as mad at Javier and Randy as he did at us.

"In the bushes." Javier said in a low tone. I remembered being young and being scared like that around the big guys.

Adam walked over to the bushes and took it out. He looked at it for a moment.

"It's fine."

We all stood there not really knowing what to do.

"Sorry." Carlo managed.

"Get the hell outta here!" Bradley's voice hadn't changed a bit.

"You should be able to trust your neighbors." Russ stated as we started to leave his driveway.

"Your name's Russ, right?"

"Yeah."

"Glad to know that, cause you're gonna get shot!" Bradley pointed his finger at Russ like it was a gun and walked back into his garage.

We walked back into Russ's garage. We'd been here almost an hour and we hadn't even started practicing. Adam held up his hand like it was a gun and pointed it at nobody in particular.

"You're gonna get shot!" he said with a laugh. He put his cymbal stand with the rest of his drum set and placed the cymbal on it.

I picked up my guitar and started messing around with the volume. Carlo picked up the microphone and held it by his side so that it wouldn't feedback. Russ didn't pick up his bass. He just stared at his amp. Eyes wide. Angry. He got like this sometimes. If he got really mad about something he wouldn't let go of it.

"I hate those guys. They're worse than the Mexicans on Barwill's street."

"Forget it," I started. "We got the stand back, let's practice."

"Dude! I'm sick and tired of it. This neighborhood, where we've lived since we were kids, it's turning into a dump!"

"So what are you gonna do about it? Today? Right now?"

"We have gooks taking over with their shops that I can't even say the names of."

Adam laughed and Carlo smiled after Russ said that.

"Like those cholos that tried to start shit with you, Tim."

"It was only one guy, Russ. The others helped me out."

"But doesn't it piss you off? Any of you?" Russ looked at Carlo and Adam. He was calming down some even though he was still furious. "It's like the minorities come here and suddenly we don't even count."

"Russ is right, man," Carlo started. "When we were kids, we could go all over. In the summer, we'd go out the door in the morning and not come back until dinner time, and while we were gone our parents never had to worry about us. It isn't like that now."

"You got people spray painting in our parks. They come here and they have no respect," Russ continued. "I'm not putting up with it anymore. I've lived on this block almost my entire life, then that White trash family moves in, they're loud and rude... who wants them here?"

"Dude, Bradley has lived here almost as long as you." I said.

"No, he hasn't. My family was on this block way before his."

"This isn't even about race anymore. It's about us." Carlo stated.

"Exactly, it's about respecting where you live."

"Yeah," Adam chimed in. "We have some people on my block like that. My dad hates them."

"So what do you guys want to do?" I asked. I don't remember the answer I was looking for, I just wanted to practice.

"Lets step up to the plate," Carlo started. "Those guys wanna party in our parks? Spraypaint our neighborhoods? Be loud and cause trouble? Fine. We have the right to do something about it."

"Exactly," Russ said. "We'll be like the new Neighborhood Watch."

Neighborhood Watch? What did we know about that?

"Look, our eyes are open to all this now... so let's keep them open. Lets make it like this neighborhood used to be." Carlo turned to me. "Tim, there's no reason why you and Erika should feel uncomfortable at a mall in your town. There's no reason why Russ and I should be kicked out of our park just because some zipperheads, who probably don't even live in our neighborhood, want to play basketball there. This isn't about being a racist. I'm not racist. It's about standing up for yourself. Defending what's yours."

"I don't know," I started, thinking about everything he'd just said. I'm bad in discussions like this mainly because I'm not really good at thinking on my feet. I always think of the perfect thing to say after the conversation's over. "I'm going away to school. I don't know how into it I am."

"Fine." Carlo turned around. "Let's practice."

"No, I mean, I'll fully back you guys up. It's just... I don't want to do anything stupid."

"So you're in?" Carlo turned back to me.

I didn't know what "in" meant. I just knew I didn't want to be out. Not with my friends.

"Yeah, I guess."

"Yeah!" Russ clapped his hands together and threw his arms up in a sign of victory. "That's what I'm talking about. This is going to be great. Things are going to go back to the way they were."

"Yeah," Carlo agreed.

"First order of business, those Mexicans at Barwill's house."

"What about Bradley?" Adam tapped his sticks against his hi-hat a few times.

"He'll get what he's got coming, don't worry about him." Russ stated sternly.

"Okay, let's practice." I said for what seemed like the millionth time. I strummed a few chords on my guitar to make sure that it was still in tune. The energy was slowly coming back. Carlo started to pace back and forth.

"Okay, check, check, check..." he said into the mic. "One, two, three... Ladies and gentlemen, we are Augmented and this first song is about having pride... it's called 'Fly The Flag'."

Then we started into the song. It sounded good. Really tight. Finally, after who knows how long, we were doing what we came here to do. I relaxed my arms and just let go. We were always at our best when we just played our instruments.

Chapter 12

The show that Isaac set up at the Macondo was great. It was cool that even when a hardcore band played L.A., as long as the show was all ages (which this one was), people from Orange County, Simi Valley and all over the L.A. suburbs would come out. Some hardcore bands had gotten shows up here with huge cover charges, they were 21 and over and nobody came. We had really lucked out at this show. The two L.A. bands had been slated to play over us. Then they showed up, started loading in their equipment and they saw that a lot of the people at the show were wearing Augmented t-shirts, so they asked us to headline. After sitting through two bad bands, the audience seemed more than ready for us. Function hadn't been able to come down from Seattle so this ended up really being our show. There were about 250 people there. Another band showed up claiming they were supposed to play and we told them they could... after us.

We were five songs into our set when a fight broke out. I have never really understood why this happens. I mean, it's a hardcore show. People pit and stage dive. If you choose to be in the pit, how can you get pissed off if someone slams into you or jumps on your head? Anyway, these two big guys were pushing each other. I saw this happening but kept playing, hoping that they would get their act together. Then one of the guys hit the other in the face. It always happens fast like that. Not that I've seen many fights. The people in the pit started moving toward them, everyone trying to get a better look. Some people tried to break the fight up. Carlo turned to us and waved his hand in the air.

"Stop playing," he said into the PA system. We stopped and he turned back to the guys squaring off in the pit. "What kind of idiots are you?!? You guys are going to get this show shutdown! I don't care about us... but a lot people drove out far distances to see all the bands play. I think they deserve that chance."

People in the audience cheered.

"You guys should have more respect for the scene."

The two guys who had been fighting in the pit continued to stare at one another.

"Are you guys done? Can we continue?"

The audience cheered louder now. The two guys were separated and the pit went back to normal. Carlo looked at me.

"Okay Tim, where did we leave off?"

I smiled because I know he knew that my hands hadn't left the frets of my guitar. He knew me better then I knew myself sometimes. Adam looked at me and came in on the drums. Russ followed. The crowd went nuts as Carlo turned back to them and resumed singing right where the song had been interrupted.

I left the show early. A lot of times after we play, some kid will grab us and try and get the band together to do an interview for their fanzine. I usually stick around, unless Erika is at the show which she had been that night. It's not that she isn't into the music or the scene, but her and Carlo have never really gotten along and she says she has nothing in common with Deborah or Lisa, so we usually split. I wish it wasn't that way, I mean who wants to have a girlfriend that doesn't get along with your best friends? Erika just thinks they're immature (which they are), but they're also my friends.

Carlo and John Barwill were out in front of the Macondo. Adam was there with his girlfriend Lisa, but they were sitting away from them, against a wall, off in their own world. Russ and Deborah walked up to them.

"Where'd Tim go?" Carlo asked.

"He left with Erika." Russ replied. Carlo shook his head. "Figures."

"Is that guy whipped?" Barwill asked with a smile.

"Barwill," Carlo started, "whipped isn't the word. That girl runs his life."

"I'm sure there are worse things... she's pretty hot."

"She sucks," Russ chimed in. "Her attitude sucks. She thinks that her and Tim should just stay at home all the time."

Deborah laughed after Russ said that. He had always treated her like she was one of the guys, so she acted like one. She wasn't girly in the typical way I'm used to most girls being.

"Yeah, she doesn't respect that he wants to do this band." Carlo said.

"But she's on stage whenever she comes to a show."

"She wouldn't even think about standing in the crowd."

"That's crazy," Barwill said laughing. "I just stopped bringing my girlfriend to shows. She's not into it."

"That's smart," Russ stated. He motioned towards Deborah. "If she didn't want to come to our shows, I wouldn't make her."

"Yeah, why come if you're not into it?" Deborah asked.

"Exactly." Carlo stared at Russ and Deborah. Carlo wasn't a bad-looking guy, and he sang in a very popular band, but he'd never had a "real" girlfriend the whole time I had known him. I wondered if it was because out of all of us he was the most serious about the band? Sometimes it seemed like it was the only thing he had.

Carlo eyed Barwill for a second. "So how are those neighbors of yours?"

"Oh, Russ told you about that? They're alright. They still have parties until all hours of the night. I was gonna call the police again, but that seems like it will just create more problems. I'd rather not even deal with it. I just ignore them and hope they ignore me."

"That sucks," Russ said, eyeing Carlo.

"Yeah, I know, but what am I going to do? Keep calling the cops whenever they have a party that's too loud? I'd never be off the phone."

"Yeah," Carlo started, saying his words slowly. "Russ and I have an idea."

"Oh yeah?" Barwill asked, "What's that? Call the immigration board?"

"No, this is better. We're gonna crash one of their parties."

Chapter 13

I sat at the table eating a bowl of Fruit Loops. My dad was slowly sipping his coffee looking over some papers from Purdue. They were the same papers he had given me a few weeks ago, but I still hadn't gotten around to really looking at them so I think he decided he would do it for me. My mom was sitting with us reading the newspaper.

"This is awful," she said as she read an article on the front page.

"What?" I asked.

"What happened to those two couples in the Orange County Canyon. I guess they were there late at night and they had some car trouble. Then these gang members pulled up and they beat up the two boys and raped the two girls."

"Really? I've been to that Canyon." Erika and I had been there a few times. It was sort of secluded and I think that's what a lot of young kids with cars liked about it.

"Well, you better be careful. I wouldn't go there anymore if I were you."

My mom put the paper down and went into the kitchen. She started fixing herself a lunch to take to work.

"So those gang members just attacked them for no reason?"

"The gang members were Mexican. They say that the people they attacked made some racial remarks."

"Like that justifies it." I was starting to get pissed. I couldn't believe anybody would even think that was an excuse.

"It's horrible. It's scary to think something like that happened here."

"Those guys should be killed." I stated. "No questions asked. Just taken to a field, lined up and shot one by one."

"Well, I don't know about that." My mom looked at me to see if I was joking or serious.

"I do. I mean, come on. You do what those guys did? No way. They forfeited all their rights to everything."

"Good thing we're not sending you to Law School."

My dad looked up from the school papers.

"It says here that there's a Boiler Gold Rush Orientation for all incoming students at the beginning of next month. Are you planning on going?" He asked. He hadn't been paying attention to any part of the conversation I was having with my mom.

"Yeah," I lied. "When is it again?"

"The 2nd through the 7th of August."

"Yeah, I plan on going. That's just a ways away."

"It's only a month. Then you start classes a few weeks after that."

We stared at each other then he went back to looking over the papers. I couldn't even think about going away to Indiana. I picked up the newspaper my mom had been reading and put it in front of me. I read the headline about the story we had just talked about:

FOUR HELD IN O.C. CANYON RAPES, BEATINGS

I stared at the pictures of the four suspects. They had blank, empty looks on their faces. It figured that they would need four guys to beat up two. These guys were punks. I wondered if they cared about anything. If they had ever been destined to be anything other than the criminals that they were. Sure they were probably remorseful about what happened, but that was only because they had gotten caught.

I continued to stare at their pictures and for some strange reason, I began to regret not fighting that cholo guy at the mall.

Chapter 14

Russ and Carlo's apartment was located close to downtown Huntington Beach. You would think that with me working so close to them I would be there all the time, but that didn't really happen. They had a two bedroom place that was sparsely decorated. It looked like they just threw old furniture in the living room area, and then they each took time decorating their own rooms even though both ended up looking practically the same. They had band pictures on the wall, clothes on the floor, records and CDs everywhere. The real difference was that Russ had a bass and a small amp in his room. The newest addition to their living room had been a velvet "painting" of Lionel Richie that they had gotten somehow. They wanted it and displayed it for no other reason then they thought it was funny.

Carlo was sitting on their worn out couch watching VH-1 and Russ was in the kitchen area eating some grillers. Carlo and I became straight edge when we were 14. Russ wasn't straight edge when we met him. Carlo had told me that since Russ became straight edge he had "broken his edge" by getting drunk a couple years ago when he and Deborah called it quits for four days. Carlo and Russ became vegetarians together just like Carlo and I became straight edge. Russ even tried to become a vegan but he couldn't do it.

"What's up, guys?" I asked as I walked inside.

Carlo looked at me.

"I just watched a Behind the Music on Milli Vanilli." He smiled.

"How was it?" I sat down on the love seat that didn't match their couch. I think this thing had been found on the corner of Newhope and Warner with a "FREE" sign on it in Fountain Valley.

"It's rad."

Russ walked over finishing up his griller. They were soy hamburgers and as far as vegetarian food goes I thought they were pretty good.

"So we're gonna meet here tonight for Barwill's, right?" He asked with his mouth full.

"Yeah," Carlo said. Russ looked at me.

"Are you coming?"

"Yeah," I said looking at Carlo and then Russ. "Also, I think I can go on tour next month for a week."

I just threw that out there. I had been thinking about it on the ride over but I hadn't made up my mind until I said it. It was probably because my dad had mentioned Purdue and I wanted to give myself other options.

"Really?" Carlo sprang off the couch.

"Are you serious?" Russ asked. His eyes were wide with excitement.

"Yeah, I thought about it. I think I can pull it off."

"That's awesome," Russ said.

"I can't wait to tell, Isaac. He's gonna be so stoked."

"Tim, this is gonna be so rad. We're gonna have such a good time."

"It's gonna rule," Carlo echoed.

"Look, I gotta get ready for work but Tim, this is awesome. We're gonna party." Russ high fived me and walked off towards his bedroom.

When straight edge guys say things like "we're gonna party" they don't mean it in the usual sense. Partying for straight edge people is like getting a group together to watch Star Wars or a porno movie. On tour, it meant we were probably going to play jokes on each other, or the other band we were touring with, or maybe break the law in harmless ways.

"That's so cool, dude," Carlo continued. "We're gonna tour. I'll find out all the dates as soon as possible." He stared at me as if I was finally giving him something he had always wanted. "I'm psyched you're coming tonight. We didn't think you would."

"Well, I wasn't too into it, but then I read this article today on what happened to those kids in the O.C. Canyon."

"Yeah, one of those kids that got beat up, his older brother is like best friends with Benji's brother."

"Really?"

"Yeah. Those guys are lucky they're in jail because Benji's brother, all those older guys are nuts."

"Didn't Benji go to jail?"

"Yeah, for like eight months. He assaulted some guy."

"That's crazy." I stared at the TV for a moment. I got an uneasy feeling in my stomach. What if I didn't go to school? What if the band didn't work out? What if I ended up like one of those guys Carlo was talking about? I hadn't really thought about that stuff much, I was still able to do everything. Now, with deciding to go on tour, and being more honest with myself about how not "into" school I was, it was as though I was making a choice that I didn't feel quite as right about as I thought it would. "Benji's not a White Power guy, is he?"

"No, he just... you know him, he doesn't take any crap off people." Carlo didn't seem to think about my question too much.

"Erika thinks he is. Remember when he was downtown that time for the outdoor show? Isaac wanted to beat him up for some comment he made. She doesn't like him at all."

"Nah, Benji was probably just being funny. Like how we all joke around. We all say stuff just to say it; because we're not supposed to. Like 'nigger this' or 'beaner that,' it doesn't mean anything. You know Isaac, he's too serious sometimes."

"Yeah." I knew what he meant because I made comments like that but only around people I knew really well, and they knew me so they knew I was kidding.

Carlo stood up.

"Lets go get something to eat. I gotta be at work at 1."

"Where do you wanna go?" I stood up as well.

"Angie's."

"Yeah dude, pizza sounds rad." I hadn't realized how hungry I was until he mentioned Angie's. Even though I eat meat, I loved just getting their cheese pizza.

We started walking out of the apartment.

"Dude, to get you even more stoked on the tour, I spoke to Isaac and our CD, only being out a month, has already sold 6,000 copies."

My heart jumped a bit. 6,000 copies. Now, I know those aren't Rolling Stones numbers, but for a local band with no videos on MTV, their only promotions being ads in fanzines and posters in independent record stores across the country, that was pretty good. And it was only the first month...

"Really? That's awesome!!"

"Lob at Blueprint told me those things are flying off the shelves. He's trying to talk me into talking to Isaac about letting us do a 7" for his new label."

We walked over to Carlo's car and started driving to Angie's. We talked about the future of the band and I forgot all about being scared, school and everything else.

Chapter 15

Russ's brother Donavon worked at a Target store and he had swiped three pairs of black workout pants, three black sweatshirts, three pairs of black gloves and three black beanies that Russ had cut eyes into so we could see with them over our faces. Sitting in the Augmented van wearing all these layers of clothing, I was burning up. I hadn't noticed summer really being that hot until tonight. Barwill and Adam were the only guys still in their regular summer clothes.

"So we're just gonna jump over the wall, light off some firecrackers...?" I asked because I wanted to know exactly what we were going to do.

"Then we'll push some people in the pool." Russ laughed.

"No, we won't." I was serious, too. I would have gone home right then if I thought Russ meant what he said. There's a fine line when you do something like this. Sort of like toilet papering somebody's house. If it's just the paper, that's one thing. You start bringing in eggs and confetti and it becomes something else entirely.

"Don't worry," Barwill looked at me. "There's no pool. It's just a big backyard. They don't have any pets either."

"Just follow my lead," Carlo said. "It'll be like when we play a show." He turned to Adam. "Dude, Adam, as soon as we hop over the wall, turn on the van. We're only gonna be about a minute."

"We gotta be quicker then that. What if they come at us or something?" I asked.

"Honestly, you guys don't need to do this."

Once Barwill said that I was half hoping someone else would agree. I couldn't. I was the one who specifically came over to Carlo and Russ's apartment earlier that day to tell them that I was in. I couldn't back out now even though I was starting to regret being there.

"Well, we are," Carlo stated. "Look, why don't you go home? We're gonna wait like 5 minutes then we're gonna go over there. We'll call you after it's done."

"Okay," Barwill said uneasily as he got out of the van. "Later. Be careful."

Nobody said anything and he slammed the door shut.

It all happened so fast.

We got out of the van and it was like watching a movie. I didn't feel like a participant at all, even though I was. It was more like I was outside myself watching everything happen. We all had our masks pulled down and Russ had given us each a pair of black gloves. Carlo held a brown grocery bag filled with leftover fireworks.

There was a brick wall between Barwill and his neighbor's house. The closer we got to it the more disoriented and out of it I felt. I wondered if it was not being used to having a mask on my face. Before I knew it, we were right in front of the brick wall. I had to put my arm out and touch it so that I didn't walk face first into it.

Russ laughed a bit when he saw me do this. I guess he and Carlo were used to wearing masks.

Mexican-type music was playing just like Barwill said it would be. It was loud but that may have been because we were so close to the backyard. I honestly hadn't heard it until we reached the brick wall. Maybe I was just looking for a reason not to be involved in all this? It was too late. We were there and it was moments away from happening. What "it" was would remain to be seen. I could now faintly hear people speaking Spanish. I felt I was slowly getting things in order but I think that was because I was standing still.

Carlo quickly opened the brown grocery bag and handed me a lighter and some firecrackers. He gave Russ a Roman candle. He took out four stink bombs. One by one he lit them and threw them over the brick wall. I was amazed at how easily he was doing all this even though he had gloves on. It seemed as though Carlo really did have a plan for what he was going to do and Russ and I were just following along. I wondered why he didn't tell us more about how all of this was going to happen?

"Light those." He said sternly, interrupting my thoughts.

I lit the firecrackers and threw them over the fence. Carlo took out two more Roman candles and then dropped the grocery bag on the grass. He lit both candles, handed one to me and then turned and handed the other one to Russ. Sparks started to fly as we set the Roman candles on top of the brick ledge and followed Carlo over the wall. I wasn't thinking right now. I was just doing and it felt good.

Looking back, I can't believe all three of us didn't set ourselves on fire going over the wall with those Roman candles.

There were some lights on in the backyard. The music was even louder now. I tried to gauge the silhouetted figures in front of us. It looked like two families. Adults, teenagers and some younger kids. "Well now that we're here what are we going to do?" I thought.

The firecrackers started to pop (even though it seemed like they had already been popping for awhile), the stinkbombs were starting to really emit smoke and the Roman candles were blazing now. Everything seemed to be happening perfectly; like this was a war movie. Something we did all the time and it was just another finely tuned mission. I could tell by the body language of the people in front of us that they were scared. They had no idea what was happening. I felt emboldened by the sense of fear that I was helping create.

"IT'S TOO LATE TO BE HAVING A PARTY!!" Carlo yelled.

In unison, it seemed, we all advanced towards them. Noises of fear were made as we did this. Some of the little kids started to cry. The smoke from the stinkbombs had filled up the backyard so much that it made it look like there were more of us than there were. Dogs started to bark. Then I remembered what Barwill said about the family having no pets and I relaxed.

"YOU DON'T UNDERSTAND?!?! YOU DON'T HABLAS ENGLAIS?!?! THEN YOU BETTER

LEARN!!! TREAT THIS NEIGHBORHOOD WITH RESPECT OR GET OUT!! THIS IS YOUR FIRST AND LAST WARNING!!!"

Russ kicked over their radio. The music went in and out for a moment then it resumed playing. I was glad that he hadn't broken it. We turned and started running toward the wall. I heard some words in Spanish that sounded like the words I'd heard at the mall. I'm sure we were being cussed at. I heard footsteps too.

They were coming after us now.

Russ and Carlo turned and threw their Roman candles at them right before they hopped the wall. I did too.

In no time it seemed like we were running across the grass to Adam as he waited in the van. The sound of the engine got louder and louder as we got closer. The van door was open and we all piled into it. Adam started to take off as Russ slammed the door shut. We all looked out the back window of the van. Some Mexican guys had come over the wall while a few others had run out of the front door of the house and were now in the street. Had we not been as quick as we were, the guys coming out the front door would have gotten us for sure.

But they hadn't. We were gone.

Chapter 16

Denny's must hate the hardcore scene. I say this because they never make any money off us. We go there a lot, usually after a show, and sometimes I'll even go there to study with Erika (though we don't get much studying done), but they probably still hate us. I say this because all we ever order when we go there are grilled cheese sandwiches and hash browns. That's it. Sometimes one of us will get a coke, but usually after a show, we'll all be so sweaty all we want is water. We also usually only leave the bare minimum as far as a tip is concerned. Now, I eat meat and so does Adam (but when he's around Carlo and Russ they give him crap about it, so he tries not to), but I really like their grilled cheese sandwiches and hash browns, so I usually just get that. Even when I come here with Erika that's all I really get.

Russ, Adam and I were sitting in a booth. Carlo had gone to call Barwill on a payphone.

"It was almost like it wasn't really happening," I said in between bites of my sandwich. "I felt like we were in a movie or something. Everything was too perfect."

"Dude, when they came after us, I swear, I thought we were dead," Russ laughed. "And then the dogs in the other yard started barking and I was like, 'Maybe Barwill didn't know that they did have a dog?!?!'"

We all cracked up.

"I could hear you guys," Adam started. "It seemed like you were in there forever."

"Yeah, Carlo just took charge, like always," Russ sipped his water.

"What was he yelling?"

"Something about learning to speak English or something."

"Yeah," Russ laughed. "He told them to respect the neighborhood. It was cool."

Carlo walked over to our booth and sat down.

"Well boys, mission accomplished." He picked up his grilled cheese sandwich and dipped it in some ketchup and tabasco sauce. "From what Barwill says, the party's over."

"Yah!!" Russ said loudly as he high fived Carlo and Adam.

"Really?" I don't know why I was surprised. We had just entered someone's home without permission and proceeded to damage their property. That would put a damper on anything. "Think they'll call the cops?"

"No," Carlo said. "Why would they?"

"Chances are some illegals live in that house. The last thing they want are the cops there." Russ stated.

"Barwill said all the noise completely stopped. He even went outside to ask them what happened, just so they'd know that he wasn't involved in it." Carlo put some hash browns in his mouth. "He watched it all from his kitchen window. He said it looked rad, like a fireworks show. He couldn't believe we threw the Roman candles at them."

Everyone laughed a bit. I smiled. We really hadn't done anything that bad and we had made a point. If there was a way to do it like that all the time, maybe we could do more things like this. The goal had been to get them to stop having their parties so late at night, right?

"What were you saying to them?" Russ asked. "Did you just think of all that on the spot?"

"I guess. Seriously, it was kind of like playing a show, only shorter. Once we started doing stuff, before we even went over the wall, the firecrackers started popping, the stink bombs were going off, we had our Roman candles lit... something just came over me. Like everything I had wanted to say to those kinds of people just started coming out. But you can't say too much in a situation like that because we had to be in and out really quick. Dude, Russ, I had no idea you were going to kick over their stereo."

"Yeah, I don't know. I mean, you were saying some good stuff. I guess I wanted to be a part of it."

We all looked at one another after Russ said that.

"Oh, you were a part of it alright," Carlo took a big drink of his water. "We all were."

Chapter 17

The middle of the week around 4 pm was usually really slow at Baha Burgers. We normally got another rush from 5 pm to 7 pm , but it had been unusually slow since I showed up at noon. It was rare but it was nice. Since we don't have a supervisor breathing down our neck, Mike and I were free to just sort of hang out. Mr. Barnes, the owner, usually showed up a few times a week to cut checks, see what needed restocking and just make sure that his restaurant was still running. I think it's cool that he trusts his employees to run the place themselves. He owns some other businesses so I think he's visiting them when he's not here.

"What's that shirt mean, man? The Tank?" Mike asked me. He was referring to the band shirt I was wearing. The Tank were in a totally different scene from Augmented. They were a "pop- punk" band and we were hardcore. We had played with them once and I thought they were good. Their drummer liked Augmented so we traded shirts and CDs. Mixed shows like punk, pop-punk, hardcore, etc., don't happen that much but they do happen. They're weird because it's like someone wrote a rule book and everyone knows their place. When the pop band plays, the people who came to see them go up to the front of the stage.

When the hardcore band plays, the hardcore kids go up front. It's sort of like everybody takes turns.

"It's a band," I said, knowing that this conversation was going to quickly turn into one of insults.

"What kind of band?"

"A punk band." They weren't a punk band but I didn't feel like explaining that to Mike.

"Ohhhh...," I could tell his "Ohhhhh" meant that he was thinking of a way to insult me. So I got there first.

"You probably wouldn't like them."

"Why not?"

"Well, for one thing, they play real guitars and drums."

"So?"

"It's not all keyboards and chimes. It doesn't sound like Depressed Mood. Sorry, I mean Depeche Mode."

"Chhhhh..., is that the only kind of music you think Asians listen to? Depeche Mode?"

"Pretty much."

"What about white people? All you listen to is Marilyn Manson and music about killing people."

"Yeah," I said smiling. "You don't know what I listen to."

"Yeah, I do. The Tank."

"You don't even know what they sound like."

"Probably sound like death metal."

I cracked up and Mike smiled.

The door to Baha Burgers opened. It was Johnny and Jeff. They're friends of Mikes. They both had hi-top fade hair styles and dressed in beach-type clothing, even though they weren't from Huntington; they lived in Garden Grove. Johnny had a Truck magazine under his arm.

"If it isn't the brothers!" Mike said. They all shook hands. "What up fools?"

"Not much. Just chillin'," Jeff replied.

Johnny held up his magazine.

"My truck is in here."

"Chhh, I told you, Johnny. How much did Duc say it was to lower it?" Mike asked.

"Two hundred bucks to cut the springs."

"What up, Tim?" Jeff asked turning to me. We shook hands. Somehow it seemed that we'd all learned to not shake hands in the traditional way but sort of just slide them into one another. When I shook hands with my parent's friends I sure didn't shake their hands that way.

"Not much, Jeff. Just hanging out with this guy." I gave Mike a playful punch in the shoulder.

"I know how that can be," Jeff said rolling his eyes.

Mike had a lot of friends and it was easy to see why. He was funny, easy going and just a general good guy to be around.

"Hey Tim," Johnny asked, "you seen my new truck?"

"Yeah," I said. "You brought it by two weeks ago when you first got it."

Chapter 18

Benji and Carlo were driving in Benji's truck. It had always amazed Carlo how many tattoos Benji had. He only had a few when they first met and now he was covered in them. He had them all up and down his arms, on his chest, his neck, on his stomach, his back and on his legs. When he worked at a hotel, he had a uniform and when he wore it nobody could tell that he had any tattoos at all. Now he had them on his hands, too. It was almost like there was no turning back for him. He had to be who he was for the rest of his life.

He and Carlo were headed north on the 55 Freeway headed toward Anaheim. Many years back it had been said that the KKK had a big presence there and the place was nicknamed "Klanaheim."

"Dude," Carlo was finishing up the story of what the Augmented guys had done. "Then we threw the Roman candles at them, hopped the wall and took off." Carlo smiled a proud smile, waiting for Benji's approval, but he didn't get anything.

"That's all you did?" Benji asked, staring at the freeway which was slowing down. It seemed like the 55 north was always crowded no matter what time of day you were on it.

"Yeah."

"Dude, that's nothing."

Carlo thought about what Benji said and stared at the road. Some days Benji was in a good mood, other days he wasn't. Today seemed like one of those bad days. It bothered Carlo that he could tell that Benji was going to react negatively to anything he said.

"Russ broke the stereo," he offered as an afterthought. If Benji didn't think them assaulting an entire family was cool, what would he care about them breaking a stereo?

"That's the best thing you've told me so far. You guys should have spray painted their house. Sprayed them in the face or something."

"That's beaner stuff, Benji," Carlo stated, mad that he had thought Russ had done the coolest thing. "That's, like, what they do."

"That's exactly why you do it to them. To show that you have the guts to put it back in their face."

"Yeah, I guess. It just went so fast. I didn't even realize what was going on."

"You can't just yell at them, Carlo. They probably don't even know English. If you want respect from people, you gotta show them that you're willing to do the stuff that they should respect you for."

"But what you're talking about sounds a little too hardcore."

Benji stared at the road, his eyes narrowing. For a second, Carlo wondered if Benji heard him. Benji's truck was loud on the freeway. They practically had to yell at one another to carry on a conversation.

"Are you frickin' kidding me?" Benji asked loudly. "Seriously, Carlo? You don't think they're just as hardcore?"

Benji looked at Carlo. A lot of times, Benji liked to joke around. Not today. Benji was always like this. Constantly inconsistent but today he seemed more angry than usual.

"Let me tell you something," Benji continued, "the other night I was driving home from the show Andy's band played."

"Guilty As Charged, yeah, they're awesome." Carlo stated. He felt good to finally be agreeing with Benji about something.

"Yeah, so it's about 12:30. I'm on Brookhurst and Talbert and I'm in the outside turn lane waiting for the light to change. These gooks pull up and there's like 10 of them in the car."

"Of course," Carlo said with a smile.

"So I look over at them and they're staring at me. Trying to look hard. So I keep staring at them and I don't change my expression." Benji stared at Carlo for a moment not saying anything. "After a few moments I give them one of these."

Benji hit his fist against his chest and extended his arm giving Carlo the "Seig Heil" sign.

"You did not!" Carlo laughed.

"The hell I didn't. So the light turns green and I pull on to the freeway. They pull up beside me and I just smile at them. They roll down their window and all of the sudden I hear, BOOM!" Benji looked at the road again and laughed to himself. "I see this flash and I slow down 'cause I don't know what just happened. So I pull over and they drive off."

"They shot at you?"

"Yeah, the pussies. They're not men. They don't fight one on one."

"Did you call the cops?"

"Hell no, I'd never call the cops. But the way I see it..." Benji paused and glanced at Carlo as if he was letting him in on a secret. "Those guys will get theirs. Especially if I see them again. I'll kill 'em."

Benji smiled at Carlo who nervously smiled back.

"When we get out I'll show you the bullet hole."

Chapter 19

"So, when do you get back from the orientation?" Erika asked as we waited in a slow drive-through line at Taco Bell.

"The 7th. It's only five days." I figured if I kept my answers short this conversation would turn into something else. I just didn't like having it, probably because I was more scared than anyone about what was going to happen when I went away to school. If I went away at all. I sort of wondered if something might happen to stop it? To make it not happen. To make everything stay the same.

"And then you go there for good four weeks later?"

"Yeah, something like that. But it's not 'for good.' I'm coming back and we'll visit each other while I'm gone, right?"

"Yeah, I just wish we were going to closer schools."

"Me too."

At the time, I don't think I realized that Erika was just as scared about all this stuff as I was.

"You think it's gonna work?" she started. "With us being so far away from each other."

"Yeah, why wouldn't it?"

"I don't know? I mean, you're gonna meet new people and I'm gonna meet new people."

"So? We don't meet new people now?"

"It's not that, it's just... I wonder what it's gonna be like, Tim. Not seeing each other all the time. Everyday."

"You don't think I'm thinking about that?"

"You don't seem like it. It's like you're going away and you don't realize how much that changes things."

"What are you talking about?" I was pissed. I hate arguing and I especially hate arguing with Erika. Maybe I wasn't giving her what she wanted. I wasn't acting concerned because I was trying not to think about all this stuff. Maybe I was too scared to tell her that. "It changes everything, but not between us."

We looked at each other now. The drive through had come to a complete stop. This was going to be one of those conversations where nothing she or I said solved anything.

"Right?" I asked, trying to reassure her as much as myself.

"I hope not." She looked out the window.

"Erika, what do you want me to do? Not do my band? Not go away?"

"No."

"So why are you making it sound like we're gonna breakup?"

There, I said it. "Break up." It was out there. I never understood why people who moved away from each other for certain periods of time felt like they had to break up, but I had never been in this situation before. I had never been this serious with a girl. "I don't know? I'm just thinking out loud."

"Well, don't." I smiled.

"Are you practicing tonight?"

"Yeah."

"Do you have to?"

"Yeah, we have a big show next month. We might go out for a week on the East Coast with Corruption. They're on tour right now, but they're going to be in town for the show. If it happens, we'd leave like the week after. They just want to check us out first. See how we play live."

"How can you do that when you're going away?"

Having her ask that made me realize that my parents reaction was going to be ten times worse.

"I'm not leaving for like six more weeks, but if my parents are cool with it, I mean, Augmented won't be making any money, but I've decided I've got to try and tour with this band at least one time before I leave. Who knows what could happen? Maybe we do really well and we can go out more? Who knows what's going to happen a year from now? The band may not even be together."

Erika was upset. I could tell by the way she was choosing her words that she was trying to keep her composure. The only good news was we were almost at the ordering speaker. I wasn't even that hungry anymore. That happens to me sometimes. I'm hungry, I don't eat, then I get a headache and I can't eat. That wasn't why I wasn't hungry now.

"So you're going to Indiana for an orientation, you're going on tour for a week...."

"Yeah?" I interrupted as if I was talking to my dad.

"What about us? Shouldn't we be trying to spend as much time together as possible?"

"I thought that we were."

A voice came over the speaker.

"Welcome to Taco Bell. Can I take your order please?"

I looked at Erika and we ordered. I got food even though I wasn't hungry.

Chapter 20

I turned off my amp and started to put my guitar stuff away. Practice was over and I wanted to get home and shower before I went over to Erika's.

"What are you doing tonight?" Carlo asked.

My back was turned and I was sorta bummed because I didn't want to hang out. I just wanted to go over to Erika's. I didn't want to deal with any "ball breaking" from my friends. I was going to be dealing with enough of that when we went on tour.

"I don't know." I started as I decided to just tell the truth. "I was gonna hang out with Erika. She's been sorta bummed because she thinks I don't want to spend any time with her. She really bummed out when I told her we were going on tour."

Nobody said anything. I turned around and looked at Carlo.

"Why? What are you doing?"

"We were thinking about going on another Augmented mission." Carlo smiled.

"Tonight?" Adam asked. He twirled a drumstick in his hand.

"No, next month, stupid," Russ snapped.

"Shut up."

"What'd you guys have in mind?" I asked.

"Beating up that guy Bradley," Russ said matter-of-factly. I had never really thought about it but Russ seemed like one of those people that went around looking for trouble. Lately there was something about him. He seemed different. Not all the time. Not much at all really. Just enough for me to notice. Like he was sort of looking forward to me going away so he could become best friends with Carlo or something.

"Dude, why do you even care about that guy? We only practice at your house once a month, you don't even live there anymore."

"So? It's still my home. And besides, he and his trailer trash friends keyed my car."

"How do you know they did it?"

"Who else would do it? In that neighborhood? On my street?"

"Come on, Tim." Carlo broke in. "You got Russ's back or not?"

"Yeah, I've got it, but why do you need four guys to beat up one?"

"Just in case there's more people. He never hangs out by himself." Russ wiped some sweat off his forehead.

"So you beat him up? What does that do? He's just gonna try and get you back."

"Then we'll get him back." Russ's tone was one of disbelief. As if he couldn't believe I was questioning his brilliant idea.

"You'll get him back, I won't."

"I know. You'll be in Indiana. Why don't you do us all a favor and quit the band now?"

"Screw you, Russ! I'm in this band just as much as you." I felt like an idiot saying that but it was true.

"Then act like you care about it."

"I do but these missions have nothing to do with our band."

"THE HELL THEY DON'T!!" Russ had a very short fuse. I wasn't scared of him or anything, but I wasn't too particularly into the idea of being the one who set him off.

"Look Tim, you don't want to come tonight, that's cool. We'll go without you. It's no big deal," Carlo said.

Russ started to put his bass back in its case.

"Should I go to my room and look for some black clothes?" Adam asked. He probably figured he'd take my spot tonight. Everybody wanted me out it seemed.

"No, just use Tim's stuff but we'll probably only have you drive again." Carlo stated.

"Oh, come on! I don't want to just drive this time!"

The guys continued talking as they broke down their equipment. All I could do was watch them. So this is how it starts? Being left out of things. Little by little. I decided that I didn't care.

Then I decided I did.

"What time do you guys think we'll be done?" I asked.

"So you're in?" Russ's tone was normal again.

"Yeah."

"That's what I like to hear."

Carlo walked over to me. He held up his hand for me to shake.

"I knew he'd come. Tim knows what side he's on."

Chapter 21

I sat in the back of the van listening. We were driving to the park in Russ's neighborhood where he figured Bradley and his friends were gonna be hanging out. I told Erika we were having a meeting at Isaac's warehouse and I was gonna be a little late. She responded with an elongated, "Okaaaay," but as long as I didn't show up too much after our originally planned meeting time, she would be cool. We were all in our black outfits but it wasn't as hot tonight. That was about the only positive thing I noticed. If Bradley and his friends weren't at the park, maybe we could just go home.

"Bradley and his friends like to drink in the park at night," Russ was saying. "They drink and smoke out. They're loud. The have pissing contests on the grass. They're like the Mexicans on the street corner in Santa Ana looking for work."

"That guy Dominic that hangs out," Carlo started, "he said Bradley and those guys sell ecstasy and speed."

"Chad Router, Bradley's best friend tried to sell E to Lisa's little brother," Adam stated.

"Really?" Russ asked.

"Yeah, he's only 11, dude."

"What a scumbag," Carlo said. He looked at me sitting in the back of the van. I just wanted to get this over with. Get my "hanging out" card punched for the night.

After a few minutes Adam pulled the van up to Stonecress Park. I had hung out here a lot when I was younger (as it wasn't too far from my house), but then it seemed like one day I just stopped going there. Sort of like I let go of something from my youth without realizing I was doing it.

Russ took out some binoculars and Carlo started to hum the Mission: Impossible theme. I smiled. Maybe this wouldn't be so bad? Russ went up to the front passenger seat and looked out the window.

"There's like four guys total. It's good because I think they're in the center of the park. Chad's there too."

"Isn't that too many?" I asked without thinking about it.

"No, because we have baseball bats." Russ continued to look out the window and I was still trying to figure out why all of this was so important to him.

"We'll be fine," Carlo said. "We're gonna swoop down on them."

Carlo looked around the van and picked up two wooden baseball bats. Russ pulled out a metal pipe that had been under the seat of the van.

"Yeah, it's gonna be like an aerial assault," Russ laughed. Carlo gave me one of the bats. It felt heavier than I thought it would.

"What are we going to do exactly?"

"We're gonna sneak into the park and surround them," Carlo said.

"Yeah, we'll each be like 6 yards apart, and when I yell 'Now!', just get up and start swinging." Russ acted like he was going to hit Adam with the pipe.

"Just be ready Adam, because we're gonna haul back here."

"Okay."

Russ opened the door to the van and hopped out. Carlo and I got out as well. The way we were going into the park, Bradley, Chad and the two other guys had their backs to us. Since they had probably been drinking, it would take them some time to realize what was happening when things got started. They were listening to some music low on a tape player. I think it was The Who. In unison it seemed, we all got low to the ground. Russ started crawling and Carlo and I followed his lead. We then spread out so that we were surrounding these guys in a semicircle. It was hard to judge if I was too close or too far from them but I did my best. It was also weird how instinctively we were doing all this. We had never practiced what we were going to do; so far we just showed up and did it. I looked over at Carlo and Russ and it seemed like they had stopped moving. In the darkness they seemed really far away and really small. I wondered if I looked like that. It was still hard to really judge anything with the mask on my head. Chad and his friends didn't seem to notice us, so I figured I was doing okay. I clutched my baseball bat hoping I was right.

I guess Russ knew when the song was gonna end because the minute it did...

"NOW!!!!!!!" He screamed.

Russ sprang off the grass with his pipe arched in the air. Carlo leapt off the grass too and I quickly followed. Maybe it was because these guys were drunk, but at first they didn't try to run or anything. They should have.

Carlo belted one of them in the chest with his baseball bat. The guy screamed and fell to the ground. Russ slammed Bradley in the mouth with his pipe. He dropped on the grass. I think he went out cold. Chad turned to run past me. We made eye contact and I clubbed him on the side of the chest. I tried not to do it that hard but I'm sure I did. He screamed and I wasn't sure what scared me more, the noise he made, the way Bradley had hit the grass or the fact that Russ and Carlo were laughing. The last guy standing tried to get away but Russ hit him on the back and he went down. Carlo then swung his bat as hard as he could and slammed their tape player about 8 feet from where it had been sitting on the table. Lights started coming on and it sounded like front doors were opening.

"LET'S GO!!!" Carlo screamed.

We all ran back to the van. I was still following my friends.

Chapter 22

The Pushing Forth Records Warehouse had attained a somewhat legendary status amongst the people in the hardcore scene. Isaac was basically "it" in terms of releasing hardcore music in Orange County. There was a cool mystique about the place. I think a lot of people in the scene thought that all the bands on the label were there all the time. Like if some random scenester just happened to come by, they could meet the people who were in their favorite bands. It didn't work that way.

Isaac ran the small warehouse and had two employees who worked part-time for very little money. They either did it for the "prestige" within the O.C. hardcore scene of working for the biggest label, or they were "down" for the Do-It-Yourself cause. Whatever the reason, Isaac ran things in a very structured way and he put in an inordinate amount of hours. All the times that I'd been there he'd been immersed in the mess that was his office. There were posters on the wall, fliers for upcoming shows, faxes, tour schedules, release dates of albums and CDs, and on top of all that there was a huge dry-erase board filled with things that needed to be done for the label. The only other help he had was his girlfriend Shayna. The two employees would stuff records, prepare CDs (Isaac didn't like paying companies to put them together for him), fill orders, silkscreen shirts and basically they made sure that the warehouse was adequately stocked with all the releases that Pushing Forth distributed. Unlike Isaac's office, the warehouse itself was very organized and clean.

Carlo sat in the office with Isaac who was half in and half out of their conversation. On the computer screen in front of him was the layout for the Tackball 12". They were a new hardcore band that Carlo didn't think were very good. It wasn't simply a case of Carlo not liking the band because they were on the same label and might steal Augmented's thunder (although that fear was always lingering in the back of his mind), it was more because none of us in Augmented thought they were very interesting. Carlo stared at the layout and wondered why Isaac was putting out a band that so obviously wasn't on the same level as some of his other releases.

"So Russ asks him straight up, 'Why don't you quit now?'" Carlo said hoping that would get Isaac's attention more and he would offer up suggestions about finding a replacement for me when I went away to school.

"And what did Tim say?" Isaac continued to stare at his computer screen. He clicked around with the mouse on his Macintosh, messing with the color tones of the album's cover.

"What could he say?" Carlo asked as he looked around the office. He hated talking to people when they couldn't give him their full attention (especially about his band), but this was Isaac so he'd take whatever time he could get. "He got pissed, but whatever. So I think that was good, because now it's kind of out in the open, but we need him to do the tour next month."

"Yeah." Isaac finally looked at Carlo. "Who are you thinking about replacing him with?"

"Benji Walker."

Isaac stared at Carlo. He didn't look back his computer screen. He wasn't sure if Carlo was serious or not.

"What?" Carlo asked almost defensively. He knew that Isaac didn't like Benji but he never knew how much he didn't like him.

"You're kidding, right?" "No, why?"

"That guy's an idiot."

They just stared at each other. It was as if Isaac forgot all about the layout he was working on. Carlo had his full attention but he wasn't so sure he wanted it now.

"He's a clown. You know he's a racist."

"No, he's not."

"Oh, he's not?" Isaac moved around in his chair a little bit. "That must've been someone else who was downtown that time I was there."

"Dude," Carlo started, "he didn't even know you were there."

"So that makes it okay? He said, and I quote, 'This place would be better if they weren't so many niggers and beaners around.' Screw that guy, Carlo. I almost kicked his ass."

Chapter 23

I stood facing my amp as I tuned my guitar. It had been going out of tune a lot lately which meant I probably had to have it intonated. At least that's what I thought it meant. Carlo stood in front of the mic which was propped onto a stand. He was holding a fanzine. The mic was on and when he spoke, without the band playing, his voice amplified loudly throughout Adam's garage. Russ was reading an article out of the newspaper. I'd seen it at breakfast that morning. I read it and then threw the paper away. It was an article on us but it hadn't been about the band. It was about what we'd done to Bradley and his friends at the park. It felt awful to get in the paper for doing something you wish you hadn't. "Dude," Russ started as he was reading it. "I can't believe I missed this."

"Yeah, my mom was reading it this morning." Adam said as he messed with his hi-hat stand.

"Do they talk about the van?"

"Not really, just the injuries."

It was good that they didn't talk about the van, that way they couldn't identify us, but I think them identifying us was the furthest thing from Russ's mind. From any of their mind's except mine. I was never really that into doing this "Neighborhood Watch" stuff anyway, but now I really wasn't into it. As it turned out, Bradley had a broken nose and his two front teeth knocked out. Chad had a few broken ribs and one of the other guys had a cracked sternum. This was assault and if the police ever did find us we'd be in a lot of trouble. Bradley had to know that it was us, or at least that it was Russ. It had been a few weeks since they had squared off on Bradley's driveway, but if Russ hadn't forgotten about it, why would Bradley?

"What do you think of that, Tim?" Carlo's voice broke into my thoughts. I pretended like I was so into tuning my guitar that I couldn't hear him. If I did this maybe he'd leave me alone. It's a horrible feeling when you don't want to be around your best friends. Since I didn't say anything, that was Carlo's cue to keep talking. "The man is in stunned silence. Maybe I'll read one of Tim's responses from the interview Augmented did in this here fanzine?"

I hated when Carlo got like this. I really wasn't in the mood for anyone today, let alone the guys in my band. It's weird how you can be so close with people, but they still anger you and make you hate them at the same time. It seemed like everything I was once comfortable with was now starting to become uncomfortable - my parents, my band, Erika...

"This is awesome!" Russ stated as he put the newspaper down. "I gotta make a copy of this. I can't believe we made the paper."

"Yes, we did, Russ. We made the paper." Carlo still turned the pages of the fanzine. His voice, especially over the PA system, was really starting to annoy me now. "I'm still trying to find something Tim said in this interview, but now I remember, he left the show early that night and surprise, surprise, wasn't a part of it."

Carlo tossed the fanzine on top of a stack of newspapers that Adam's parents kept in the garage to recycle.

"When are we gonna go out again?" Adam asked eagerly.

"Soon, young Adam. Very soon." Carlo was trying to sound like Obi Wan Kenobi.

I checked the last string on my guitar, or at least I acted like I was. I had finished tuning awhile ago, I'd just postponed facing the guys until I couldn't stand it anymore. Right then, I just wanted to play the songs and get out of there.

"Okay, let's practice."

"Ladies and Gentlemen," Carlo's voice echoed a bit now, "Tim speaks!"

"What do you guys want to play first?" I asked, ignoring him. Maybe if I could push this practice forward, we could play the songs and I could leave?

"Why are you in such a bad mood?" Russ asked as he slung his bass around his neck and turned his amp on.

"I'm not. I just want to practice. I have plans later."

"What are you doing?" Carlo smiled.

"What do you think he's doing? He's playing house with Erika?"

"Shut up, Russ. Are we gonna practice or not?" "Sure, Tim." Now Carlo was mad at me. "Your attitude sucks. Let's just play the record."

"Okay." I placed my hands on the frets to make a powerchord of C. "Are you guys ready?"

Everyone seemed to nod their heads and we went into the first song. I didn't really look at Carlo or Russ for the rest of the practice, but out of the corner of my eye I saw them looking at me and then at each other and I knew they were thinking the same thing.

For the longest time it seemed like no matter what happened between us: insults, arguments, whatever... none of it mattered because we had the band. We always had the band. Now things were starting to get more serious and it didn't seem like just having the band was going to make things okay anymore.

Chapter 24

I don't know when it started but for some reason I no longer enjoyed eating with my parents. It wasn't because I didn't want to tell them about the tour. I think it started when I began working and wasn't home as much. Then I began going out with Erika pretty seriously, Augmented started happening and most of my college classes were at night. So it had now reached a point where all of us eating together was pretty rare. It seemed like I would go weeks, maybe even months, without eating with them. Breakfast was tricky because morning was the one time when we were all home together. I usually got the tail end of that, though. I would come downstairs and start eating and then shortly after that they would both leave. One might think that when we were together it would be great, we could catch up, but I found myself having less and less to say to them; or at least to my father. I always thought that when you got older it got easier to relate to your parents because you had experiences that made you understand each other more. Well, I was older now and so far it hadn't been like that.

"I took care of getting you your plane ticket for the orientation," My father said.

"Okay." I was trying to eat fast so I could go back up to my room. I had an idea for a song I wanted to work on. I even had lyrics, which was rare. Carlo could be a real jerk when other people came up with lyrics but if he thought they were good he would use them. He just didn't like being told how to sing the words. My only problem was I couldn't be creative on an empty stomach and my parents were hanging around the kitchen longer than usual that morning. Otherwise, I would have tried to wait until after they were gone to come downstairs.

"Are you excited about school?" My mom asked.

"Yeah, I guess."

My parents looked at each other. They were going to be spending a lot of money to send me off to school, and "Yeah, I guess" was probably not the answer they were hoping for. I sort of hoped they might already know that I wasn't too happy to be going away. I was reaching a point where I wasn't able to avoid this stuff that much anymore. It seemed like the only way I could was to lock myself in my room and play my guitar.

"Are there any schools around here I could go to? I mean there have to be other schools in California that are just as good as Purdue?"

"I'm sure there are... but we thought you wanted to go away?" My mom asked cautiously. This had obviously been something that they discussed amongst themselves, and unless I emphatically stated that I didn't want to leave, they wouldn't really believe me. And then if I did admit that, they wouldn't want to believe it.

"I do, it's just... I mean, maybe I can still go away to some place near here? This way I could still do the band. I could be closer to Erika."

"Do the band?" My dad's voice was a mix of contempt and disbelief. As if he couldn't understand why I took my band that seriously. If he only knew...

"Yeah, things are going really well. We're selling a lot of records, I mean..."

"Tim, do you know how hard it is to make it in music?"

"Yeah, but if it wasn't hard, it wouldn't be worth anything to do it."

"Why don't you just focus on school? Get your degree. Get a good job. Then do your band."

"Dad, do you realize what you're saying? I'm young now. I'm in a popular band, now. Who knows what we can do? If I don't at least try this, I think I'm gonna go my whole life regretting it."

"So you're saying you're not going away to school?" My mom's voice sounded a lot like my father's now.

This was it, though. I could change everything if I just said "Yes." If I told them I didn't want to go away to school. I wanted to go part-time, work part-time and do the band full-time. This would be the moment, if I could just tell them. If I could make them understand.

"No, I just think that if I stayed around here, I can do both. I mean, if the band doesn't work out, I'm still in school. I just don't want to give up on it."

"Tim, I don't understand you." My dad was starting to get angry. "You've been preparing to do this for a long time. Everything is all set up."

"Dad, other than music, I don't know what else I want to do with my life. All I want to do is play my guitar." That sounded so stupid, I wished I hadn't said it but only because I think it made me look bad; like a little kid.

"But Tim, that's not going to get you anywhere. Do you know how hard it is to be successful in a rock band? It can take years. If it happens. All these groups that are big now, they've been doing it forever. Your group is big in a small scene, that's all."

It's hard to categorize punk or hardcore music or to explain to people why you're straight edge if they're not involved in the scene. It's just something in you. You feel things differently or certain things mean something to you in a way that they just don't to those on the outside. Anyway, I stopped talking during this conversation and just listened. There was nothing else I could say to explain why I felt the way I did, or why I thought my music, my band and my scene was different. I was still going away to school and I hadn't mentioned anything about the tour.

Time was getting shorter.

Chapter 25

Like most couples, when you first start going out, Erika and I had had our share of sex. That first year we were together, it was like we couldn't keep our hands off one another. After three years, I was still very attracted to her, both mentally and physically, but we didn't have as much sex now. I think we still did it on a weekly basis (sometimes more then that), but our relationship had progressed, it seemed, and then it plateaued. I was going to try and count how much sex we had over a 6-month period but then I figured what was the point? We were together, we loved each other, but we'd both never been in a relationship as serious as this, so who knew what to expect? What scared me was I sort of didn't know where we were going any longer.

Like my parents, Erika's both worked. The difference was, where my dad was sometimes home a decent amount during the day, Erika's parents were never home until about 5 O'clock. She had an older brother and an older sister but they had moved out a couple of years ago. This meant we had her entire two-story house in Anaheim to ourselves. Her house looked a lot like mine. It was very neat, organized and everything seemed to be in its place.

I laid against her in bed and kissed her soft shoulder. I stared at her skin for a moment and wondered if she wasn't

Mexican would she still be this brown? Was her skin darker because she was out in the sun a lot? I think a lot of weird, random things.

"Deborah told me that you, Russ and Carlo beat up some guys in a park."

She just blurted it out. Like she'd been thinking about it all day. She had been doing stuff like that a lot lately, and the only reason I noticed it was because it had really started to bother me.

"She did?" I was as shocked as I sounded. Then it occurred to me that this stuff Augmented was supposed to be doing in secret, wasn't a secret anymore. If I hadn't been so surprised I think I might've worried about who else knew. If Russ wasn't keeping this a secret, I doubt Carlo was either.

"Yeah, she also said that you guys broke into some Mexican people's house just because they were having a party."

"She told you this?" Man, I was doing a great job of defending myself, wasn't I?

"Is it true?"

"Well," I was trying to figure out the best way to explain this. "We didn't break into anybody's house. And as for those guys in the park, they had it coming."

"They deserved to be beaten with baseball bats?"

"No, I mean..."

"That's what you just said."

It was quickly dawning on me that we were going to get into this. I knew I was going to be a jerk. I was going to say a lot of bad things and come off like I was mad at her, when the person I was really mad at was Russ.

"No, look, it's hard to explain, but do you remember how things used to be in Orange County? Like when we were younger? This place was perfect. It was the best place to grow up, but if you look around, it's not like that anymore. It's different."

"So that's why you guys did what you did?"

She turned to me now. It was strange to be in front of her, both of us naked, covered only by her blanket and wonder how she might react if I touched her? I couldn't believe I was thinking like that.

"Is it just minorities? Or do you guys attack everyone?"

"Okay Erika, you got me. I'm a racist. You've been my girlfriend for the last 3 years, but I'm prejudiced against you."

"Don't turn this around."

"I'm not."

"You are. Tim, what you guys are doing is wrong. You really hurt those guys in the park. I can't believe that you would be a part of a hate group."

"We're not a hate group. We're not even a group. We're a band. Look, I just went along with those guys because I grew up here. This is my home and I want to protect it."

"From what?"

I hated being questioned like this. She knew I hated it too which also meant that she didn't care.

"From people who are gonna mess it up. From people that have this need to vandalize property by spray painting their stupid gang names everywhere, or selling drugs, which is what those guys in the park do, Erika. It's like that cholo guy at the mall... we're trying to hold on to what made our neighborhoods great..."

"You're lumping everyone together, Tim. What gives you the right to do this? What makes you special? Because you're White?"

"Oh okay, this is a race thing? I'm White, so I'm this privileged person. I don't deserve anything anyway? Erika, you're about as Mexican as I am."

"Why? Because I don't fit into your stereotype of what a Mexican should be?"

"No, because you only seem to care about your ethnicity when you can get mad about something."

I got out of the bed and started putting my clothes on. We only said a few words to each other before I left.

Chapter 26

The following account is what happened one night when Carlo, Russ and Adam went out without me. As I wasn't there, I don't know how accurate this is, but Adam, who would tell me everything later, had no reason to lie.

The evening began with the three of them hanging out in Carlo and Russ's apartment watching TV. Carlo had tried to call me because they wanted to go out again. The big problem, unlike before, was they didn't have any reason to go out. They just wanted to go out and find one. I was out to dinner with my parents and Erika, and at that time, I was doing my best to only hang out with those guys if we were practicing or playing a show. I still had a lot to work out with Erika and my parents as far as going away and going on tour, and I half planned to bring these things up at dinner. I didn't, though. All we talked about was the schools we were going to, where we were going to be living, what courses we were going to take, etc.

"Tim's not answering." Carlo put the phone down.

"What do you want to do?" Russ asked, turning his attention away from the TV.

"Maybe we should just hang here out tonight," Adam offered.

"Shut up." Russ said tersely.

"I'm gonna call Benji." Carlo dialed the number as he said it.

"Dude, yeah. That guy will be so much more into it than Tim."

As it turned out, I would be very glad I couldn't hang out. Not that it would matter much.

The guys plus Benji had all decided to go to one of the newer strip malls in Irvine to eat. South Orange County, areas like Irvine, Dana Point, Mission Viejo, Aliso Viejo, etc., were considered the really nice areas of O.C. North Orange County where I lived was nice but it's sort of like how Las Vegas is set up. Where I was would be like downtown and a place like Irvine was the strip. There were a lot of Asians there. UCI, the University of California, Irvine, was often jokingly called the University of Chinese Immigrants. I don't know whose idea it was to go to Irvine that night, but I don't think the guys just ended up there.

They sat in the parking lot of an In-N-Out Burger, with the side door to the Augmented van open, eating their burgers and fries. The In-N-Out was located across from a row of different types of places to eat. There was a sandwich shop, an Italian eatery, an Indian restaurant and a bakery all snugly packed together in that one area.

"So what do you guys want to do?" Russ asked.

With Benji there, Carlo noticed that Russ seemed bolder than ever. Like no matter what he did or would do, Benji had his back. On top of this, Russ talked to Benji in such a way that it seemed like with every word he said he was trying to impress him.

"I had a run-in with some gooks a few weeks ago," Benji stated, his mouth full of food. (Later, Adam would confide to me that he thought Benji was "sort of gross.") "I've been looking for them."

"Think they're gonna come here?" Carlo asked as he picked out all the good fries from the bad ones in his order.

"I don't know. I hope so."

"Are those the guys that shot at you?" Russ asked.

"Someone shot at you?" Adam couldn't fathom something like that happening in O.C.

"Yeah," Benji eyed him slyly. "What do you think of that, little man?"

"That's messed up."

Benji stared at Adam for a moment. As if he was trying to figure out something to say back.

"Yeah, it is," Benji started. "These people come here with their guns and their bullshit lowered cars, they travel around in packs..."

"A million to a house," Carlo chimed in. Russ laughed.

"You know what, little man? They could put all the niggers, beaners and gooks in a big park, they could blow it up, and I'd celebrate."

"What about the Habeebs?" Russ asked.

"Of course them!" Benji snapped and smiled. "Kikes, Sandniggers, whatever... put them all in the park. Make one big stew of shit and watch it go BOOM!"

Benji smacked his hands together to emphasize his point. He cracked up with laughter. Russ and Carlo laughed as well. After a few moments, Benji glared at Adam again.

"What do you think of that, little man?"

About 20 minutes later Benji sat half-in and half-out of the van smoking a cigarette. Russ and Carlo skated around the parking lot. Adam laid in the back of the van, staring at the lights of the parking lot through the back window. Every so often he looked at Benji and wondered how a guy who was 24 could look so much older. So worn out and beaten. Adam never wanted to look like that.

A truck pulled into the parking lot. It was "tricked out" with loud, house music reverberating through its tinted windows. The trucked belonged to Johnny Le. This was the same Johnny that I knew through working with Mike Nguyen. With Johnny on this night was Quan Tran. He looked over at the Augmented van, then at Carlo and Russ on their skateboards, and decided to park across from them by the other restaurants. Benji stared at Johnny's truck as Carlo and Russ skated up to him. He spit on the ground, a few inches away from Carlo's board.

"Hey!" Carlo half laughed.

Johnny and Quan got out of the truck and started walking into the Italian eatery.

"Why you going in there?" Benji yelled. "They don't serve Mack Lock Gin." He was imitating the way he thought Asian people talked. We'd all done that before but never to their faces. Johnny and Quan were aware that they were being stared at, but they didn't seem to notice what Benji had said. They went inside the eatery.

"Are those the guys?" Carlo asked.

"I think one of them is." Benji's eyes were wide with excitement about a possible confrontation.

Russ started skating in a wide circle around the parking lot. As he got close to Johnny's truck he discreetly spit on it. He skated back to Carlo and Benji hoping they'd seen what he did. They were still watching Johnny and Quan inside the eatery.

Johnny and Quan ordered their food and then sat down next to the window so they could watch Johnny's truck. Every so often, they glanced over at Carlo, Benji and Russ. Johnny took out his cellphone and started calling someone.

"He's probably calling his friends," Carlo laughed.

"Let's make a move then." Benji got up.

"What are you gonna do?" Russ asked.

"Whatever I do, back it up."

Adam sat up in the van. He had been listening to what the guys were saying but he didn't seem to understand what was happening.

"What's going on?" He asked.

"Get out of the van, little man." Benji wasn't even looking at him. He was already on his way over to Johnny's truck.

"Get out, Adam. Grab a bat." Russ said.

Benji continued to walk towards Johnny and Quan. As he did, he took out a key and ran it across the entire passenger side of Johnny's truck. Benji stared directly at him as he did this.

Johnny watched in disbelief. It didn't seem possible that somebody could be doing this. It didn't even really register when Benji finished keying his car, smiled, and then gave them both the finger. Benji turned around and walked back to Carlo and Russ. Benji wasn't even walking fast. Adam thought it seemed like he wanted those guys to catch him. To put their hands on him and give him a reason (in his mind) to kill them.

"This is gonna be great!" Russ said with nervous laughter.

Johnny and Quan ran out of the eatery. Johnny pushed Benji who didn't see that he had discreetly slid on a pair of brass knuckles.

"WHY'D YOU DO THAT TO MY TRUCK, FOOL?!?!" Johnny shrieked.

Benji turned around and punched Johnny in the face as hard as he could. Quan reached around and got Benji in a headlock. Russ ran over and started punching Quan as hard as he could in the back of the head. Carlo ran toward Johnny but he grabbed Carlo by the throat and cracked him in the face.

People started to gather around now. Without thinking, Adam grabbed a baseball bat, ran across the parking lot and slammed Johnny (who was trying to help Quan) in the head with it. His body slumped to the ground; unconscious.

"I thought I killed him," Adam tearfully told me later.

Benji, Carlo and Russ ganged up on Quan. They beat on him with everything they had. Three against one. They kicked him and took turns punching him until he was a bloody mess. Benji grabbed the bat from Adam. He walked over to Johnny's truck and smashed the tail lights, the windows and whatever else he could hit.

"LET'S GO! LET'S GO!" Carlo yelled.

They all ran back to the van. As they did, Russ turned to all the people watching and raised his fist in the air.

"AUGMENTED CREW!! GO BACK TO WHERE YOU CAME FROM, GOOKS!!" He yelled and then jumped into the van.

Quan started to sit up a bit. Only now did some of the onlookers come to his aid. The Augmented van whipped out of the parking lot and drove away.

The realization of what they'd just done had yet to kick in. As Adam drove he had to remind himself not to drive too fast. He didn't really comprehend what he'd just been involved in but it was something he never wanted to be part of again.

Russ and Carlo hid the bats and pipes under some band merch (mostly t-shirts and hoodies) so that if they got pulled over and a cop glanced into the van, they wouldn't be able to see them. Benji took off his brass knuckles, wiped the blood on a black Augmented t-shirt and put them back in his pocket. Carlo stared at him and Benji smiled.

"That was so rad!" Russ said loudly. He was still amped up. They all were. "Where'd you get those brass knuckles, Benji?"

"What brass knuckles?" Benji asked sternly; then he smiled again. "I don't even know what those things look like."

"I can't believe we just did that." Carlo stared out the back window. He couldn't really see anything except the glare of the streetlights, but he wanted to see if anyone was following them. He didn't remember how everything happened, he just knew that it had happened. Benji had told him once that when he got in fights, sometimes he wasn't able to see anything for a few moments when it was all over. As if you were so in the moment that when you got out of it, you had to readjust your vision so you could see everything normally again.

"Yeah, well you all better keep your mouths shut and start acting like nothing happened. They might be able to identify us." Benji was as cold with them as he had been with Johnny and Quan. Carlo always felt that Benji didn't care about friendship or how well he knew someone. If you crossed him, he'd let you know it and you'd better be prepared to fight about it.

"You don't think they can, do you?" Adam nervously asked.

"You better hope not. I didn't see many people with pencils and paper taking down the license plate, but then again, I was busy doing other stuff." Benji laughed a bit after he said that.

"Dude, who cares? That was awesome." Russ laughed.

"That was crazy," Carlo stated. "We're not telling Tim about this, okay?"

"What? Why not?" Russ wanted to tell everyone even though Benji said he couldn't.

"Because we're not. He won't understand. Don't say anything, okay Adam?"

"Okay," he replied vacantly.

"What won't that pussy understand? Those slopes got what they deserved." Benji sat back relaxing. He fixed his gaze on Adam. "Little man, good going with the bat."

"I only hit him once. Not hard."

"That was pissed what you did. Keep it up."

"You don't think I really hurt him, do you?" Adam's voice almost cracked a little. He was starting to get really scared. It was almost hard to drive. He had always loved to hang out with the older guys and be the drummer of such a popular band, but this was the first time he wished he wasn't around any of them. That he didn't know any of these guys.

"I hope you did hurt him," Benji stated matter-of-factly. "I hope you killed him."

Russ couldn't help laughing. Carlo smiled.

"That was so nuts. Benji, you think those were the guys that shot at you a few weeks ago?" Carlo asked.

Benji sat still for a moment. Thinking in the darkness of the van.

"I don't know if it was them. Who cares if it was or wasn't?"

Chapter 27

The guys seemed more withdrawn than usual. Augmented often practiced how we played live. Some people say bands shouldn't do that, that you'll waste it all in practice, but we had always believed that you "play how you practice." The set list was posted on a dry-erase board on the wall, but I misread where we were on it which was why I went into "Fly The Flag" instead of "Despised." This was a song Russ had written and I thought it sucked. That wasn't why I had messed up playing it though.

"I thought we were going into 'Despised' next?" Carlo asked as Russ and Adam stopped playing. Adam was more withdrawn than any of them.

"Okay," I said, glancing at the set list.

"Dude," Russ started. "Would you liven up?"

"Shut up." I said. I didn't want to get into it with them and I also didn't think I was being any "less lively" than they were. It seemed like no matter what I did or what they did, we were always a little bit off. We used to sort of be that way but we'd always been on the same page as far as the band was concerned. It wasn't like that as much now.

"Come on, Tim. Get into it," Carlo started. "How are we going to tour with you acting like this?" Anyone eavesdropping on our practice would say it sounded more like group therapy than it did a hardcore band.

"I'm just tired."

"You been up late, huh?" Russ started to do a "bump and grind" with his bass. The other guys laughed. "Look, let's just play."

Without waiting for them to agree, I went right into "Despised". Thankfully, they followed me and we could avoid an argument. I figured once we got on the road everything would be okay. I could relax then. I pressed my fingers hard against the frets of the guitar, closed my eyes and just listened to the sounds. Russ was really out of tune. He rarely would tune before playing. He just took his bass out of the case and started going. I thought about stopping the song and telling him but I just wanted to play. Even if he was out of tune, he wasn't about to cop to it. He might've before, but he was much more standoffish now. It was as if the bigger Augmented got, the more his ego went with it. Carlo was the same way.

Maybe I was, too?

I was the first one done breaking down my stuff. I picked up my guitar case and started walking out of Adam's garage.

"Where are you going?" Carlo asked. "I thought we were gonna hang out?"

"I can't. I'm going to that orientation next week, so I gotta spend some time with Erika."

"We're not going out tonight. We were just gonna be mellow and hang out our place. Watch a movie or something?"

"That's cool. I gotta bail. I'll call you."

It wasn't that warm out and the cold air felt good after being in Adam's garage for two hours. Normally, we practice for three, but nobody seemed to complain tonight when we just sort of stopped after two. I saw the guys looking at me and talking as I drove off.

"Do you believe that?" Carlo asked Russ incredulously. "Maybe he should ask his girlfriend if it's okay to still be in the band?"

"I say we cut him, dude." Russ ran his finger across his throat. "Tour or no tour."

"We'll, I've been jamming with Benji," Carlo said hopefully.

"Can he pull it?"

"Yeah, he can play the songs. He's not as tight as Tim, but he's pretty good for having just listened to the record and figured the songs out."

"Benji's gonna be in the band?" This was the first Adam remembered hearing about it. He suddenly got a sick feeling in his stomach. If he could help it he never wanted to see Benji Walker again.

"Dude, that'd be so rad if he was in the band." Russ put his bass in its case. In his mind, I was already out of Augmented. He was on tour and not looking back. "We could tour, just do the band. That'd be awesome."

Chapter 28

Today was one of those rare days when I was working the register at Baha Burgers alone. Mr. Barnes didn't like to have two people working if he could help it. It didn't usually work out that way but as summer slowly started to wind down, he tried mixing up the shifts as much as he could. Since most of us were college students and lived at home with our parents, we didn't mind.

I gave a good-looking mother who was with her daughter a to-go order. As I did, I couldn't help but wonder if Erika would look like that when she got older. As the woman walked out, Mike and Johnny walked in.

I should've known something was wrong by the way that they came toward me. They basically stormed into the place. Johnny had a bunch of bruises all over his face.

"Hey, what's up?" I looked at Johnny. "What happened to you?"

"What's up with you and your friends?" Johnny was very pissed about something. Mike gave me a look. It's weird when you're used to joking around with someone and then things suddenly get serious. It's even worse when they talk to you about something they're mad about and you have no idea what it is.

"What are you talking about?"

People in the restaurant were starting to look over at us now. Our voices were rising with each sentence and for some dumb reason, I still thought the guys were joking around with me.

"You and your boys, Tim." The fact that Mike was starting to yell in the place that he worked meant that he was mad at me too, and he didn't care if someone complained to our boss and he lost his job over it. Slowly, I got a faint idea in my mind. Not an idea so much, just names...

Russ, Carlo and Adam.

They had done something without me.

"What? I didn't do anything?"

"Don't lie about it." As surprised as I was, Johnny's tone was starting to piss me off.

"Lie about what? I didn't do anything."

"Don't lie, Tim." Mike's tone was bordering on anger, disbelief and hatred. I had never seen him close to anything like this. He was always so laid back. Nothing ever bothered him. "You guys keyed Johnny's truck, then you jumped him, man. Quan's in the hospital."

"Look, I didn't do anything. I don't even know what you guys are talking about."

"Chhhh, man..." Mike continued to stare at me like I was some kind of punk trying to get something over on him. I hate talking to people and trying to convince them of something, especially when no matter what I say it isn't going to matter. It's how I feel most of the time talking to my dad.

"I swear, I didn't do anything. If something happened with any of my friends, I promise I wasn't there."

"You and your boys better watch yourselves." Johnny mad dogged me.

"Look, don't threaten me. I didn't do anything."

I couldn't believe I was actually having this conversation with these guys.

"All this time, man. All this time. Behind my back." Mike shook his head like I'd let him down.

"You say you weren't there, fine." Johnny stated. "But when we find your friends we'll see if they were there."

"Johnny!" I was almost beside myself. Two customers came in. "Why would I be a part of something like that? You're my friends. Don't you think if I was there and anything like that even came close to happening I would've stopped it?"

The two people behind Quan and Johnny were staring at the menu. I don't think they had any idea that I was arguing with the two people in front of them.

"Quan says that after you jumped him, you guys yelled 'Augmented Crew.' That's your band, right? Told him to go back to where he came from. Called him a gook!?!" Mike's voice was getting even louder.

"Look, you guys have to believe me. Don't do anything, let me talk to those guys."

At this point the two customers looked at me. They wanted to order. Right now, I couldn't think of anything less important. Mike started to walk out of the restaurant.

"Tell your friends to watch out." Johnny eyed me carefully to make sure I knew what he meant. These guys weren't in a gang but they had friends that were, which meant that they weren't going to leave it to the cops. They weren't going to file charges of assault or vandalism for what my friends had done to Johnny's truck. They were going to settle this their way. These guys were nice but they were also tough.

Johnny turned and started walking out of Baha Burgers. Mike looked back at me one more time and shook his head.

Working the rest of the shift was awful. I could barely focus on anything. I got orders wrong, I gave back incorrect change... I couldn't believe that my friends would do this. There had to be some mistake. Maybe some kids had read in the paper about what we'd done so they tried to copy us? I didn't believe that. Even though everything was changing, had things changed that much? Had they changed to the point that Carlo, Russ and Adam felt they had to do what Mike and Johnny said they did?

I pulled up to Carlo and Russ's apartment and was half hoping they weren't home. I really didn't want to argue with them but I had to do something. I got up to the front door and just walked inside. Russ was making himself some macaroni and cheese while Carlo sat in front of the TV writing lyrics into a notebook covered with band stickers. For a second, I found that odd because we hadn't written any new songs but I wasn't here to talk about that.

"What the hell did you guys do?" I don't remember if I yelled or not but I probably did.

"What are you talking about?" Carlo looked up from his notebook.

"Last week, when I didn't hang out. What the hell did you guys do?"

"Nothing."

"Look, don't lie to me. I'm working today and my friend Mike and his friend Johnny came in. They say you guys keyed his truck, jumped Johnny and his friend Quan, yelled 'Augmented Crew' and then called them gooks?!?!"

Russ laughed. I shot him a look. I was so pissed. He had not one ounce of remorse. I hated him right now. I hated all these guys.

"What were you guys thinking?" "Dude," Carlo started, his relaxed tone unchanged. "Things just got a little out of hand. Benji was there..." "Great! So he's a part of this now?" "Look Tim, you weren't around. Why do you even care?" Carlo sat up.

"I don't believe you!! You could go to jail for what you did. You could've killed those guys."

"Tim, relax," Russ said.

"Yeah, Tim! They kill people every day. Come on, man, have some balls. We made a statement. A real statement this time. Not just kicking over a radio at a beaner party. These guys think they're so cool, they drive around in their bullshit lowered cars, listening to nigger music pretending to be gangsters. They shot at Benji a few weeks ago. Screw those guys. I'm stoked we did what we did."

"Dude, what if those guys shot at your mom? Or shot Erika?" Russ asked.

"You guys are so messed up."

"Yeah?" Carlo sprung off the chair and moved toward me some. "Why don't you get a little messed up? You can't because you're living at home with mommy and daddy who are sending you off to school so you can be a number. A statistic on the chart of the middle class. Well, forget it. I don't want that. None of us do."

"Oh, yeah, you guys have it so hard. Russ' parents pay his rent and he works in their warehouse. Whoa, that's really struggling."

"Don't make comments about me. I'll kick your ass."

"Shut up."

Russ moved toward me now. I tensed up a bit. I had come over here pissed but I never thought about physically fighting these guys.

"You wanna go, dude?" He was about a foot away from me.

"Look," I started, "I'm out. I'm not doing any of that stuff anymore. It's stupid. You guys are doing it all wrong. You're no better than the people you think you're fighting against and you're not even fighting against the right ones."

I walked out of the apartment. I thought about warning them that Mike's friends were gonna retaliate but I decided not to bother. These guys wouldn't care anyway. It wasn't until I was about half a mile from the apartment that I wondered if I still wanted to be in the band anymore.

Chapter 29

The next day I called Erika. She was more distant than normal and on any other occasion I would've talked to her some other time, but I hadn't talked to anybody about what Russ, Carlo, Benji and Adam had done and I wanted to. Only, I got the impression that Erika didn't want to talk to me. I told her I was gonna come to her house, I'd take her out to eat, or maybe we could go to the movies. She told me not to knock on the door but when I got to her street she'd come outside and meet me.

"We can talk in your car." She said.

I had no idea what was going on but I figured I'd work it all out.

Erika had been waiting outside for me.

"Why won't you talk to me inside your house?" I asked as she got in my car. She was even more distant now. She didn't even seem like she wanted to be near me. She just sat there and as I stared at her face I realized she'd been crying. A lot. "Erika? Why can't I talk to you inside?"

"Because I don't want you in my house."

A cold wave went through my entire body. What had I done to make her say that?

"What?" I half thought I would get a different answer.

"I know what happened." She said in a measured tone. She was on the verge of tears, which actually didn't bother me because at least if she was crying she felt something, right? "Deborah told me everything."

I felt like the biggest idiot. I had no idea what to say. My only defense was that I hadn't been there, but for some reason I figured Erika knew this and it didn't matter.

"If this is about Carlo and them beating up those Asian guys, I wasn't there. If you remember, I was with you until 11 that night then I went home."

"Come on Tim, do you really expect me to believe that?"

"Yes, because I'm telling you the truth." I was getting angry which made me sound more defensive, but if my own girlfriend didn't believe me... this was awful. "Look, I don't know what Deborah told you but did I lie about any of the other things I was involved in?"

"I just can't believe it. I can't believe you guys. It's like this whole time we've been together you've been laughing at me. Thinking I was less than you are."

"I have not." This was an awful conversation to be having. I loved Erika. She was beautiful to me. She was a beautiful person. I didn't care what she was. I couldn't believe she really thought that I felt that way about her. "Erika, if I was a racist, why would I be with you? If I thought I was better than you why would we have been together for three years? I can't believe you think that way about me."

Then, she looked me dead in the eyes.

"That makes two of us."

"So nothing I say right now matters? You don't care that I wasn't even there?"

She shook her head as she wiped some tears from her eyes.

Then it hit me.

It was over.

"Erika, I don't believe this. So..." My body went cold again. A lump was starting to constrict my throat. "You're breaking up with me?

More tears came down her checks as she nodded her head again.

"I'm sorry. I just can't be with you anymore. You've tainted everything."

I sat there not believing this was happening. Not believing that Erika had just said what she said.

"Say something, Tim."

"There's nothing for me to say." I didn't recognize the sound of my own voice it was so low. I wondered if she even heard me. "I mean... I can repeat myself over and over, but if you don't want to believe me...."

Then I realized I was crying. It had been so long since I'd cried about anything, I almost didn't remember what it felt like. As awful as it would be to lose Augmented it wouldn't even compare to what it would be like losing Erika.

"I love you, Erika. I always have. I'm just so confused right now. I guess we started doing those things, I did them... because we wanted things to be the way they were, but they're not that way anymore. Everything's changing. Everything's changed. I just... I wasn't there, Erika. Not that night, I swear. I just can't believe you think this way about me."

We sat there and after a few moments she got out of the car without saying anything. I just stayed there.

Alone.

Chapter 30

The next few days I just went through the motions. I got up even though I didn't feel like it. I went to work even though I didn't feel like it and I even practiced my guitar, which I really didn't feel like doing. I had heard through some of the cooks at Baha Burgers that Mike had set up his schedule so that he would be working the days when I wasn't. Then there was talk that he was even looking for another job. I came home one night and remembered my parents had gone to a play in Laguna Beach so I went to Taco Bell.

The place wasn't that busy. As I walked in I glanced around at the other people in the restaurant and placed my order. There were Whites, Asians, Mexicans and Middle Eastern people eating and talking. It seemed that only now I had really started noticing things like this. For years I had just lived in Orange County and everyone and everything was the same. Now, for no reason at all, all I saw were people's differences.

"Number 27." I heard a voice call.

I walked up to the counter. A young kid, whose name badge said Aaron, held my order out to me. He was White. I gave him my receipt.

"Would you like some hot sauce?" he asked. He smiled at me a little bit as if he was thinking something.

"No, I'm fine." I took my order. I was gonna look through it, to make sure they'd gotten it right, but I hated when people did that to me at Baha Burgers.

"You play in Augmented, right?"

"Yeah."

I get recognized from time to time and it's really cool but in hardcore you're not supposed to make too much of it. It's supposed to be something that separates our scene from all the others. No Rockstars. Yeah, try telling that to Carlo and Russ; even Adam sometimes.

"You guys are rad."

"Thanks. My name's Tim."

We shook hands.

"I know. When are you playing again?"

This was an eager kid who had probably only recently started going to shows. I was just like him a few years ago. I still thought I was like that. Sort of.

"August 13th at Club Royale."

"Awesome."

"Cool, I'll see you there."

"Yeah." He said. I turned and started walking away. "Is it true you guys beat people up?"

I turned and looked at him. How in the world had he found out what we had done?

"Who'd you hear that from?"

"I don't know. Some friends of mine heard you did."

"Well, it's not true, we didn't do anything."

"I was gonna say, that's pretty cool if you did." He smiled.

"Yeah," I said, staring him straight in the eye, "well, we didn't." I probably came off like a jerk but I wasn't really thinking right anyway.

"That's cool, I just thought I'd ask."

"I'll see you at the show."

"Yeah, you will. Later Tim."

I walked outside. I stopped for a moment and threw my food in the trash.

Chapter 31

I went to Indiana for a week for the Boiler Gold Rush Orientation at Purdue and I hated it. At first I thought I might really enjoy getting away from everything. Truth be told, I was sick of Orange County. I never thought I would feel that way but I did. Then the minute I got to Indiana I realized I didn't want to be there either. I felt awful. Why was I doing any of this? Everything about the trip felt forced. Forty minutes after I got there I was sitting in the back of a large auditorium listening to some students as they stood at a microphone, making jokes and talking about the school. They were a "Welcoming Committee" of some sort, trying to make all the new students feel comfortable and at home. Everyone was laughing. They all wanted to be there it seemed.

I barely spoke to the person they had me rooming with for the week (I'll bet he went home and had a lot of great things to say about me) and on the third day I ditched out of a sporting event and went for a walk.

What made all of this so strange was I knew what was bothering me, but all I wanted was for things to be like how they had been. It seemed like it had only been 6 weeks before that everything was great. Why couldn't I just go back to that? I kept walking. Wondering. What would happen to my band? To Erika? Would she start dating other guys at UCLA? Was she seeing someone already? What would happen to me? Would I just go on with my life? Would I go away and come back and all Orange County would be to me would be the place I used to live? Just streets, homes and buildings? I didn't know how people moved on and started new lives but they did it.

Somehow during all of this thinking, I hadn't noticed that I was crying. I couldn't help it. I slowly laid down on the grass, covered my face and just cried. I didn't know if anyone was around, or if anybody saw me, and I didn't care. I didn't plan on being here in the fall anyway. I think it was at that moment that the realization hit me.

There was no point in trying to get everything back to normal.

In trying to make things how they were, what had been (or how I thought things had been) was in the past and there was nothing I could do now. Maybe I had taken certain things for granted, maybe I hadn't, but the way I remembered things was gone. Just like that and there was no getting them back. All I had now were memories.

I would have to start all over.

I was making it all sound a lot easier then it was because truthfully, I was scared out of my mind about where things were headed. About where I was headed.

Eventually, I picked myself up off the grass and walked back to my room. The sporting event was still going on and I was glad to be alone because I couldn't stop crying.

Chapter 32

Carlo followed Isaac around the Pushing Forth Records Warehouse. Isaac was pulling orders because they had recently gotten slammed and one of the normal warehouse workers was sick.

"So is he still in the band?" Isaac asked. Carlo had been complaining about how I had been acting lately. Isaac had always wondered what would happen to the band once I left (this was all stuff he told me later; maybe that was why he had been so involved in talking to Carlo about my replacement?). He signed us knowing my intentions, but he also thought that if the band did really well that might change things. He had been right but nobody could ever foresee that things would get this complicated. In Isaac's mind, without me, Augmented was just another average hardcore band with a good frontman.

"Yeah, I guess," Carlo said, "but we've been practicing with Benji."

Isaac stared at Carlo to see if there was anything in Carlo's face that would tell Isaac he wasn't serious.

"Tell me you're kidding."

"I'm not. He's in the band. We're gonna start practicing with him and Tim and we should have two guitarists soon for our live shows. Maybe even for the one on August 13th."

"Carlo," Isaac was almost beside him himself, "he's a racist."

"He's not a racist, he's just proud."

"He beat up two Asian guys for no reason."

"No, I was there. You know what those guys did? They shot at him about a month ago on the 405."

"You were with him when he beat those guys up?"

"Yeah, we were just hanging out. Then those gooks showed up..."

"Whoa...," Isaac glared at Carlo and didn't say anything so he would know Isaac was serious. "Don't talk like that around me. Ever. What's wrong with you, Carlo?"

"So these guys show up and Benji tells me that they're the ones who shot at him. I mean, dude, what do you want him to do?"

"He carries brass knuckles and mace. He's a puss. I can't believe you'd have that scumbag in your band."

"I thought you and him were friends before?"

"I've never been friends with Benji Walker. He's a punk."

Carlo looked around the warehouse. Isaac could tell by Carlo's body language that this was clearly a conversation he didn't think they'd be having. Carlo probably figured that Augmented was doing so well that it didn't matter who was in the band. As long as they kept selling records Isaac would put them out.

"So you don't think he should be in the band?" Carlo asked absentmindedly.

"Have you even been listening to me? You think Corruption will take you on tour if he's playing in your band? Those guys hate him more then I do. He stole money from them when he worked their merch booth. Everyone hates him. I can't believe you'd even consider having him in Augmented."

"What do you want us to do?" Carlo was pissed but he also knew his anger act wouldn't go over well with Isaac. Augmented needed him. For now, anyway. "You know we need someone to take Tim's place if we're gonna tour and fully do the band. It's gotta be someone that we know; a bro. You know this... you were the one telling us that we needed to do this!"

"Dude Carlo, there are a million other guitarists that would love to play in Augmented." Isaac felt bad because this wasn't just business. He liked Carlo and didn't want to bum him out but at the same time having Benji in the band was a dealbreaker. "Look man, it's your band, so what I think isn't important, but I'm not gonna put out Augmented records or support you guys in any way if he's in your band."

Chapter 33

Russ and Carlo sat in the living room of their apartment and watched TV. They really weren't paying attention to it, it was more or less a soundtrack for whatever was happening in the room.

"So we can't be on his label if Benji's in the band?" Russ asked.

"Nope." Carlo stared at the screen. He was so pissed he wanted to call Isaac up right then and say they were off the label. How could he tell them they needed to put more into the band and then when they tried he qualified it by saying who they could or couldn't do it with? In Carlo's mind, Isaac had no say in any of this.

"Screw that. He can't tell us who we can and can't have in our band." Russ said, seemingly echoing his thoughts.

"You're right. He just won't put out our records."

"We'll get on another label."

"What other labels are there? In Orange County. Isaac is it. He's the biggest."

"What about New Dawn?"

Carlo hated having this conversation. The bands that seemed to do the best were the bands like Corruption. They didn't jump from a mid-size label to another mid-size label, they went from smaller labels to bigger labels until they finally ended up on a larger independent label that was a subsidiary of a major. Augmented looked like they were well on their way to doing that. Now, it seemed just the opposite. If they switched to New Dawn, all the kids who wrote for fanzines and on the Internet would start talking and asking things like, "Why was one of the biggest O.C. hardcore bands no longer on the biggest O.C. hardcore label?" On top of that, New Dawn represented a step backwards because no matter how Carlo thought about it, Pushing Forth Records was much bigger than them.

"They're on the East Coast." Carlo felt this was the best argument against it.

"So?" Russ didn't understand.

"Dude, we gotta be on a label that's local. That's why Isaac is perfect, because he's right in our backyard. What about when we play locally and we need merch? New Dawn would have to send it all the way from New Jersey. That sucks."

"They're pretty big, dude. Look, Isaac is the biggest label around here but there are other labels we could be on. Smaller labels but they'd probably do more for us." Russ stared at Carlo. "I mean dude, we sold 5,000 7"s, and I know our CD has sold a lot, and we haven't seen any money from it."

"We also spent a lot to record."

"No Carlo, Tim spent a lot to record. We did all our parts just fine. He's the one that took all the extra time, remember? What about our tour with Corruption? What's Isaac doing for that? Is it even happening?"

"Look, I don't even wanna think about this anymore." Carlo was hungry and he wanted to make himself something to eat, but he seemed destined to remain in this conversation in which there weren't going to be any answers.

"So what are we gonna do?" Russ was starting to get mad. He didn't care. In his mind, Augmented was big everywhere.

"I don't know."

"When does Tim come back?"

"Tomorrow. I'm picking him up from the airport."

"Are you gonna tell him about Benji?"

Carlo couldn't help smiling.

"Yeah, I mean, he's gonna find out anyway."

"What do you think he's gonna say?"

"He'll probably be bummed but whatever, I mean, we all want to do the band. What can he say?"

For some reason, Carlo started to relax. He slowly got up and went into the kitchen. He just wanted to do his band.

Chapter 34

I pulled open the passenger door and sat down in the front seat of Carlo's car with my bag in my lap. We drove away. There wasn't really much traffic at John Wayne Airport today (there never really was) and I was glad.

"Did I miss anything while I was gone?"

"Nah, things were pretty mellow." Carlo replied. We drove in silence for a few moments. It was awkward. "Hey...," he started, "how come you didn't tell anyone that you and Erika broke up?"

"I didn't really want to talk about it. I still don't." I thought of asking how he had heard about it but I didn't care.

"Okay," he said, his tone implying that I was being a jerk, and I probably was. "What would you think about Benji playing second guitar in the band?"

I had known this was going to happen. I even sorta knew that Benji was gonna be the guy they were gonna try and replace me with.

"That sucks," I said matter of factly. Everything was going down in flames around me, I might as well go with it. They were gonna do whatever they wanted regardless of how I felt, so I saw no point in not being honest. Carlo looked at me trying to decide if I was being serious or joking. I just stared at him. "We don't need a second guitar player."

"No, it's just... this way we could still do stuff while you were gone. You could both play and then when you leave, he could take over until you come back."

"Does he even know how to play guitar?"

"Yeah." Carlo perked up, thinking he was selling me on the idea. "He knows all our songs, too. We jammed with him as a full band last week."

"You're already practicing with him?" Why this surprised me I had no idea, but it did.

"Yeah."

"So he's in the band?"

"Yeah... I guess."

That did it. Carlo had probably been nervous. After all he was the one in Augmented who had known me the longest, which is probably why he was the one who had to tell me about Benji.

"Tim, what do you want us to do? You're going away, you don't hang out that much anymore, I mean, what are we supposed to think?"

"I don't hang out?" We were now having two conversations with neither of us saying what the other wanted to hear. I sorta wondered if I told him how much this band meant to me, would it even matter? I decided I didn't want to know the answer.

"We're all trying to do this band," Carlo said. "We all want to give it 100%, except you. That's fine. You go do your school thing and we're gonna do ours. We're all really serious about this, we're gonna start touring..."

"So you're kicking me out of the band?"

"No, not at all. We just... we really want to go for it and you don't want to."

"Go for it." I hated that term. What did it mean? I always thought we were going for it by being involved in hardcore. By not being like all the other bands in scenes that were "going for it."

We continued talking after that but I don't really remember too much about the conversation. I just knew that as far as my life was concerned, things were going to get a lot worse before they got better.

Chapter 35

I was in my room playing my guitar through a tiny practice amp. I had played through the entire Augmented set and now I was working on some newer songs. I had decided that I wasn't going to quit the band. I wasn't going to do anything for that matter. I was just going to sit back and let things happen. I realized that my life was pretty solid for a long time. Now it wasn't. Trying to make things how they used to be would only end up making them worse. Believe me, I knew a thing or two about that now. Trying to do that would only make everything shift and change again. So the best thing I could do would be to do nothing, at least until things slowed down. All these changes had to end. I kept telling myself that anyway.

I just practiced my guitar. I'd been doing that a lot since I returned from Indiana. I'd go to work (I still hadn't spoken with Mike), come home, close the door to my room and play my guitar. I figured if I didn't have anything else, I would at least have this. I wanted to talk to Mike but I had to get him alone. Around his friends he wouldn't listen to me. I felt if I could just talk to him, I could make him understand that I had nothing to do with what happened.

The door to my bedroom opened and my dad walked in. I had been avoiding my parents. Mainly my dad, but my mom ended up being thrown in there as well.

"So, let's talk about your trip," he started. I turned the volume down on my guitar but I didn't stop playing it.

"Can we do it later?"

"Come on, Tim. You've been home almost a week and you haven't spoken to us. Did you not like the campus?"

The campus? I barely remembered anything about it.

"It was fine. Look, I'm trying to practice my guitar. Can we talk later?"

"No, Tim. We're gonna talk now. We're gonna have a long conversation about your attitude."

I started playing my guitar again. I even turned up the volume. I knew I was being stupid.

"Tim, stop! I'm not gonna talk over you!!"

I continued strumming. My dad moved toward me. For a second, I thought he was going to hit me. I couldn't remember the last time he did that. He turned my amp off.

"There, now what's your problem?"

"I don't have a problem. It's everyone else that has a problem with me."

"Look, your mom tells me that you and Erika broke up..."

"I'm not talking about this with you."

I put my guitar down and walked out of my room. My dad followed after me. I didn't want to act like this but I couldn't help myself.

"You better grow up, Tim." My dad's voice echoed after me. I felt like such an idiot having one of these talks right now. "Life isn't just your little world."

I walked into the downstairs front area of my parents house and turned around.

"My little world is my life!" I yelled. "And right now, I don't want to talk to you about school, my future or anything else, because to you, my world outside of that isn't important."

I was squaring off against my dad. We had argued and yelled before but this was different. I had nobody to back me up. Nobody to go to. Not my mom, Erika, the band. Nothing.

"So you don't want to go away to school? You want to stay here and play in your little band?"

"My band isn't little. I could go on tour with my band. I could see the world. People like my 'little band.' People care about the things I'm doing in my 'little band.' What have you ever done?"

I said it. There was no turning back. Right or wrong this was how I felt.

"Well, Tim," my dad was mad but I could see he had been surprised by my response. He was no longer talking at me but to me. "Look around you. You live a pretty good life. You're a rock n' roll star that doesn't pay rent, doesn't pay for food, doesn't pay for anything you have!"

"I'm 20 years old! I'm doing the best I can! What do you want from me!?!?" I screamed.

My mom came up from the living room area that was located in the small downstairs part of our house.

"Would you both stop yelling?"

"Tim," my dad continued, "I want you to realize that this moment in your life, when everything seems so important, it is just one piece of something bigger. You have a future if you go to school. What kind of future do you have with your music?"

The future? Who cared about the future? That was what I wanted to say. I couldn't because I didn't know what I thought. I was however scared of a future without Augmented, without Erika... I was really scared about that. I then wondered what would happen if I brought up the possible Augmented tour? I'd almost forgotten about that.

"Who cares!?! Why does everything have to be about my future? Why can't I just do something that I love?"

"Because it's not getting you anywhere."

"YOU DON'T KNOW WHERE IT'S GETTING ME!" I shrieked. "You don't know anything about my band!! You call it 'rock n' roll' but you've never seen us!! You don't even know what kind of music we play!!!"

"Don't yell at me! Who do you think you're talking too!?!?" My dad was yelling louder than I'd ever heard him yell in my life. He had to try and assert himself. There would be no winners in this argument but he certainly wasn't going to lose.

"Who do you think YOU'RE talking to?" I yelled back. "Yeah, you've made a nice home. Thanks. Now go retire and die. I guess that's the plan. Well, I'm not doing that. This is my life and I'm gonna do what I want to do."

"Not while you're living here."

I stared at him for a moment not saying anything. I didn't care anymore. I had nothing. Who cared? Who really cared anymore? Everything was out in the open. With Augmented, school, everything.

"Fine, I'm gone."

I stormed out of the house. My mom called after me but I got in my car and took off. I didn't know where I was going. I had nowhere to go and I didn't care.

I had to get away from my parents. Nothing they would say, no talk we could have was going to solve my problems. I felt helpless. Like everything in my life was going in one direction, and I was going in another. It was awful because nothing I was doing seemed like it was making my situation any better. I was trying, believe me, I was trying to get a handle on everything but maybe that was my problem? This was a bad time. A really bad time that I just didn't have any clue about how to deal with. I had never had things in my life fall apart like this. I'd always considered myself lucky when I saw other people having the problems that I never had. Now I wasn't so sure that I'd been so fortunate. Maybe I'd have been better off having more problems in my life, instead of having them all dumped on me at the same time.

I pulled into the left-turn lane at an intersection. Next to me were two Mexican guys in a lowered car. They were listening to hip-hop music. It was loud. Too loud for me right now.

BOOM-BAH-BOOM...

Their speaker system seemed like it was rattling not only their car but mine as well. Mike had once told me that it sounds really loud outside the car, but inside the car it's not that loud at all. I remember wondering why it had to be listened to that way but I never got around to asking him. Now I probably never would. That was just another thought on top of a million other thoughts that were making me miserable.

The windows to the loud car were down. So were mine. I looked at the guys in the car and the driver looked at me.

"Yeah...," I said in a low voice as I looked away. "I can play loud music too."

I turned on the CD player and the Corruption disk came on. I turned it up full blast. It sounded awful. It was too loud and distorted through my speakers at such a high volume.

"HEY!" the driver yelled over the music, "TURN THAT SHIT DOWN!"

"WHY DON'T YOU TURN THAT SHIT DOWN?!?!" I stared straight into his eyes. These guys could beat the crap out of me. I wanted them too. It would give me something else to think about. Maybe Erika would take pity on me? I could get her back? Maybe this was all I needed to see that Carlo, Russ and Benji were right? I could make everything easier on myself if I just thought like everyone else.

"WHAT DID YOU SAY?" The driver asked.

"YOU HEARD ME, BEANER!!"

Both of the Mexican guys glared at me.

My light thankfully turned green. I looked at the guys and turned left. Cars across the street were turning left on their arrow so the guys couldn't after follow me. They yelled a few things and in my rearview mirror I saw them give me the finger.

I kept driving. Faster and faster. I still had no idea where I was going. I just knew that I hated those guys. I hated all of them. All the Mexicans and Blacks that had ever gotten tough with me. All the gooks I had to listen to as they spoke in their weird languages that made no sense. I hated all the stores with names I didn't understand. All the people that were different from me who were poor and cultivated their ghetto culture.

I hated them all.

At that moment I realized that I had probably always felt this way. I just never knew it until right then. I had always thought I was above these people; even Erika. I loved her but I always felt like I had something over her. Like she was lucky to be with me. That I was somehow superior. When did this start? Had I always been like this?

I kept driving and thinking. Strangely, for the first time in a long while it seemed like things were finally starting to make sense. The problem had been me all along. And as scared as I was about what this meant (especially now that I knew this), for some reason I felt like I was going to be okay.

I had been the problem. And I didn't want to be it anymore. I didn't want to be anything except me.

I was still really scared but I was gonna be okay.

Chapter 36

"Hey, look who it is," Isaac said with a smile. When he smiled I relaxed a little bit. I knew that we were still cool.

"Hey Isaac, what's up?"

"This is a surprise. Most of you Augmented guys haven't been lurking around here since I put your last record out." He smiled.

"Well, you know us," I started, smiling as well, "Once we get what we want we're kinda done with you."

Isaac cracked up.

"Yeah, you guys are like that." He turned and started walking into his office. "Come on in."

I suddenly felt very good about coming to see Isaac.

I sat across from Isaac who was at his desk. On the computer screen in front of him was a layout for the band Function. They were doing a split 7" with another band on the label. They were from Seattle and Isaac mainly put out Orange County hardcore bands, but there weren't any rules for that or anything. He had a put out a rockabilly band a few years ago called The Dusters. They were some friends of his from high school. They stood out like a sore thumb in his catalogue and didn't sell very well, but nobody seemed to think it was that odd. Pushing Forth Records was Isaac's label and he could do what he wanted with it. That was the great thing about not being corporate owned or having to answer to anybody. Some major label a few years ago had tried to get him to sell out to them (even offering him somewhere in the neighborhood of $2 million dollars) but he said, "No." That was the story anyway. I'd never asked him if it was true. I didn't figure it was any of my business.

I had always been impressed with how "hands on" Isaac was with his label. He needed to make shirts, but rather than pay to have some company make them, he bought a silkscreen press and taught himself how to do it. He needed designs and covers for the bands he was putting out, so he bought a Macintosh computer and a Photoshop program. Then when he got really good at it and was too busy, he hired employees and taught them how to do it. A lot of them became better than him at silkscreening and designing layouts, he'd say. Through hardcore these people were developing skills that they could use in other areas. A few people who quit working for Isaac got really high-paying graphic arts jobs. What made all this even better was that when these people were learning this stuff, they had no idea how valuable it would be. It was all done simply out of a love for the music and wanting to be a part of something. If I didn't go away to school, maybe I could work for Isaac.

"I don't know what to tell you, Tim." Isaac was really focused as he talked to me. Usually, he was doing a million things, but not now. I guess he felt this was an important conversation. "If it was me, I'd quit."

Isaac looked at me as if he was making sure I understood what he was saying. It seemed strange that he and I had never really gotten to know each other, because there was something about this conversation that felt good. Like Isaac knew that I was a smart guy. That I wasn't like Carlo and Russ. I respected him and he respected me. He also was the first person I had spoken with that really understood how confused I was.

"Do you really want to be associated with that?" he continued. "Carlo thinks Augmented is going to be so big but you get a reputation for being involved with White Power, whether you are or not, it doesn't matter. If kids start writing in their fanzines and on the Internet that Augmented is a racist band, it doesn't matter if it's true or not. It's true as far as anyone that doesn't know you is concerned. And right now, at the level the band is at, nobody really does know you guys. I mean, you can forget about touring with Corruption."

"I know, I kinda figured that. It's just, we've worked so hard." I looked at Isaac because I could feel myself starting to get emotional. I had no control lately it seemed. "That's what's so confusing. This shouldn't be happening now. I thought all I wanted... all we wanted was to play in this band."

"You're going away to school aren't you?"

"Yeah, but that's a whole other story." I looked around the room and wondered what it might be like working here.

"You don't want to go?"

"I don't know. The only thing I do know is that nothing makes me happier then playing in my band. At least that's how it used to be. I'm just scared that if I don't give it a shot, I'm gonna go my whole life regretting not giving this band 100%. But now that all this other stuff has happened... when it all started, the stuff we did actually seemed like it was for a good cause."

I felt so stupid after I said that.

"What cause is that?" Isaac leaned back in his chair.

"We wanted... this is gonna sound dumb, but I guess we wanted to protect our neighborhood. It's changed so much and I guess cuz' we're all getting older, I think that scared us. We felt left out."

"Left out of what, Tim?" He leaned forward. "Who do you think you're protecting the neighborhood from? The Mexicans? The Vietnamese? The few Blacks that can afford to live where you guys do?"

"No, you see, that wasn't it. It was like we were protecting it from people that want to mess it up. From people that don't respect other people. Race really wasn't the reason..."

"It's just that most of the people happened to be other races." He stated.

We stared at each other. I had no argument and I wasn't arguing anyway. The last thing I needed on top of everything else was to piss Isaac off.

"Look man, protecting your neighborhood from vandalism is one thing. But the way you guys were doing it didn't differentiate between being protectors and being a hate group."

"Well, what do you do? Things are changing, places that you lived next to all your life are no longer nice. There isn't a respect like there once was."

"How do you know this?" Isaac wasn't yelling but his voice was stern. "Do you ever talk to any of these people? Did you ever think that maybe it's because you're getting older? And you're noticing all these changes because you're the one whose changing?"

Chapter 37

"You want anything else with that?" I heard Mike ask a customer.

I walked out to my register and started getting it ready. Baha Burgers was dead today. I had been surprised to see Mike working the same shift as me.

"No, I'm fine. Thank you," the customer said as they walked away.

Mike stared out at the eating area as I finished preparing my register. Normally, he would tell me to "hurry up" and call me a "lazy white boy." It's funny how when you're friends with someone you can make fun of them about their race or anything else, almost. But if you're not friends or you don't know somebody that well... you can't say that stuff. It seems like it would be the other way around. You wouldn't call the people that you know names, but it doesn't work like that.

"Hey, Mike," I said.

He didn't look at me but just sort of raised his head in acknowledgment. I decided to go for it.

"Look man... I'm really sorry about what happened, but you have to believe me. I wasn't there. I would never have had anything to do with something like that. And if I had been there, that never would've happened." Mike still didn't look at me. I decided to keep going. "I'm being serious, Mike. No joking now. I'm not a racist. I mean, we joke and we make fun of each other, but I could care less what you are. I don't want to be like that and I don't want you to think of me that way."

"Why you sorry then?" He finally said. "If you had nothing to do with it?"

"Because I know the people who did it and I think it's wrong."

"They're people in your band, right? They're your boys."

"Yeah."

"And you're still in the band with them, right?"

"Yeah, but I'm not like them. Look, it wasn't always like this. I'm sorry, man. I'm sorry about what happened and I'm sorry your friends got hurt. I wanna talk to Quan. I want to apologize to him."

"Why would he accept it, man?"

"Maybe he won't but I just want to try and make this right before it gets out of hand and becomes something I can't stop."

"Like what?"

"I don't know?" He still hadn't looked at me. "Look, I consider you a good friend of mine. We've been working together... I'm not a racist." I extended my hand. "And I know you're not one either."

Mike looked at me. He smiled a bit but his eyes were still serious. He didn't trust me anymore.

After a few moments he shook my hand.

"Chhhh, when you wanna go see Quan?"

Chapter 38

I walked up to Club Royale holding my guitar. Russ had brought my amp with the rest of the equipment in the Augmented van. I hadn't really spoken to any of the guys other than Carlo since I'd been home. I half wondered if I was even playing the show. Like I might show up and Benji would be on stage and they would no longer need me. It seemed like forever since we'd practiced. We had been practicing for this show since before I left for Purdue, so I just sort of assumed it was still on. We had played here so many times, I kind of instinctively just knew when to show up.

When I first started going to hardcore shows, Carlo and I would always show up early for the first band. Sometimes it was cool but most of the time it sucked because nobody really shows up for the opener. That's why a lot of show fliers say they start earlier than they really do. No band wants to play to nobody. This is where the term "punk rock time" came from. Anyway, the more I started to go to shows, the more I realized that if I only wanted to see the headliner, I'd show up for the third band on a four- or five-band band bill. Carlo, when Augmented first started, used to lecture us about how we had to support the scene and show up for all the bands, but as we got more popular he stopped feeling the need to be there for every one that was playing. Sometimes, he was now the last person to show up. Tonight, that was me.

In spite of all the crap going on in my life, I forgot about it when I saw the line around the corner of the packed club. The band Victim was playing. I had bought their 7" and thought it was awful. They were nice guys, though. That's one cool thing about hardcore- you can suck, but if you're nice and if someone in your band "works" the right people, you can get good shows. Victim's drummer supposedly "jocked" Carlo (meaning he was always on him about our bands playing together) which is how I figured they got on this bill. I didn't even know what label they were on.

I felt sort of stupid walking up with my guitar case. People looked at me and said "Hi," "Augmented," or called out the names to some of our songs. I don't care who you are, if you play in a band you gotta like being recognized like that. I passed by Benji, who was sitting in the back of his truck. His girlfriend Sonya was leaning against him and a bunch of other guys were standing around them. Sonya was really tall for a girl and she had short, black, bobbed hair. She would have been really pretty if she didn't have so many tattoos and a ring in her nose. Most of the guys had shaved heads, tattoos and wore tank-tops. Benji and I made eye contact but that was it. He had always been cool to me before, or at least decent, but now he seemed like he didn't have to be. Like even though I was still in the band, he was sort of taking my place so he didn't have to put on an act anymore. I thought he would have been cooler seeing as how technically we were bandmates now, but whatever. I walked up to the side door where the bouncer was standing. He knew that I was in Augmented and he let me inside.

The sight of the girls on the side of the stage wasn't lost on me. Deborah, Lisa and now Sonya stood watching us as we got ready to play. Had Erika and I still been together, she probably would've come to the show and she would have been standing with them. Now, she didn't have any reason to come anymore, but I did look around a little for her. I tuned my guitar as Adam checked his drums in the monitors. There were more people than ever in the club tonight it seemed. Bodies were packed against the stage and while I was excited to play in front of this many people, I was nervous. I wished we had been able to practice more. I finished tuning.

"I'm ready," I said to Russ. The guys in the band all seemed different. Like they had moved on and I was an outsider now.

"Okay," he said. He had recently shaved his head. It looked okay.

I started to take the stance I take when we play. It's comfortable and it makes it look like I am moving around a lot even though I'm not. All my muscles tensed up like always. Maybe I could play my problems away?

"Wait!" Adam said, "The banner!"

"Oh yeah," Russ started to look around the back area of the stage. "Hey Benji, we need the banner."

Benji and one of his friends, a skinhead, got on stage and moved behind Adam. They put up a white on black banner that said "Augmented Crew" on it. In the middle was a crowd of people with their fists in the air. Under that it said, "Til Death." People in the audience started to cheer. It seemed like all of them were. Benji looked at Russ and laughed as he and his friend walked off stage.

Out of nowhere it seemed, Carlo appeared. All of this was like a rehearsed play that I wasn't in on. People cheered again as he took the microphone. It always amazed me how "done up" he got for our shows. He always got his haircut, wore a new shirt and just seemed to take on a whole new image. I never really thought about this until tonight. Man, I was tired of not noticing things until I noticed them. I almost wished I could be immune to everything, then nothing could change, and if it did, it wouldn't matter to me because I wouldn't care anyway. But you can't be like that, even if you want to. And despite how bad I felt, I didn't want to be that way.

Carlo took the mic off the stand and put it behind Adam like he always did.

"Good evening everyone!" Carlo started. "It's been a crazy summer and it's only gonna get crazier."

The crowd started to cheer. Russ went into a bassline, I clutched my guitar and realized this was the first time ever that I had to think about what song I was playing. People started moshing around the pit area.

"This first song is for Benji Walker, the newest member of Augmented. It's called 'By My Side.'"

Adam smashed down on his drums and we all came in. The pit area erupted with people. Bodies went everywhere.

They were stagediving, pitting and aggressively singing along with Carlo who didn't even have to move to get people excited now. Everything seemed heightened, the response was more intense than it had ever been. Like everything was leading up to this show.

I let go a little bit and fell back into being in the band again.

We had moved into "Someday." It was one of our heavier songs. When I first wrote it, none of the guys in the band really liked it and they didn't think it was an Augmented song. I knew that it was and when we first played it, the response was so good, Russ and Carlo actually apologized for telling me that they wouldn't play the song.

Carlo stood at the front of the stage with what seemed like 300 people pressed against him. We were at a point in the song where he repeated the same line over and over.

"I'll never be like you/I'll never be like them"

The more he said it, the more the song builds up behind his words. It was like the entire club was singing along with him and moving to the rhythm of the music. I looked out into the crowd. At this moment, nothing mattered. Everything might be fine. With Erika, the band, school, my life was going to be fine. I was going to be okay. I felt normal again.

I continued to look out into the crowd. There were a bunch of skinheads in the pit. These were people I had never seen before. Not that I know everyone at our shows. Hardly. These guys just looked different. Like they'd been somewhere else this whole time and they'd just come into the scene for this show. Don't ask me how or why I thought this, I just did.

The more I stared at them, I noticed that some of them would hit their fist's against their chests and then raise them in the air. They were moving their mouths and singing along.

Then it slowly dawned on me that that wasn't what they were doing.

As more of them hit their fist's against their chest, I realized that they were saying "Seig Heil."

"Seig Heil."

The music kept coming from my band. Picking up in tempo. Instinctively. How this was happening I had no idea, I just knew that somehow I was a part of this. That I had inadvertently been a part of it. From the time I'd agreed to go over to Barwill's neighbors house.

The people in the pit weren't moving together anymore. They were slamming into one another violently. A few of the skinheads had taken over and they were just throwing themselves around. Augmented fans, people who had come to the show to see us, just watched them. They no longer felt comfortable enough to enjoy our music the way they wanted to. It seemed like the more I watched this, the more people I saw raising their fists in the air and saying, "Seig Heil." I recognized some of them from outside of Club Royale. I had seen them hanging around Benji's truck.

The music kept going but it was unimportant now. It was just background noise for these people. These few people that felt that Augmented thought like them, so they supported us. I continued to play the song but I wasn't moving around at all now. After awhile, I turned and faced my amp. Russ, Carlo and Adam hadn't seen anything that I'd seen at the show that night. They just saw more Augmented fans.

"I think I'm quitting, Carlo." I said matter of factly as I finished loading my amp into the back of my car. Carlo and I were in the middle of the parking lot. Russ, Adam, Benji and a bunch of Benji's friends were in front of Club Royale putting the rest of the equipment into the Augmented van.

"Yeah, I figured that." He said with an easy going smile. He stared at me for a moment to make sure I knew what he meant. It was strange staring at someone I no longer knew. "It's cool. I knew something was up when you asked to take your amp home instead of having us take it to Adam's house."

I laughed a little bit.

"Yeah, it's just... I'm going away to school. You guys already have Benji in the band."

"Yeah."

"It's just better if I quit now. The tour's off, we don't have any other shows set up. Plus, I don't want to hold you guys back from doing the things you want to do."

"You used to want to do those things, too." We looked at each other after he said that and it seemed like we had faintly connected again. But it was just for that moment. Almost like we had seen in each other the people we used to be. "But we all knew you leaving was going to be a problem."

"I can't tour full time and I know you guys want to do that."

"It's cool, dude," Carlo said casually. He was over it. I think he was just glad that me leaving the band had been easy. They wanted me out and I wanted out, so it wasn't like they would look bad to the scene. Like they had kicked me out. Even in this alternative scene, sometimes a bad breakup can start rumors that really hurt a band. "Tim didn't want to be in the band anymore. He was going off to school" is what I would read in the interviews in fanzines and on the Internet.

"Okay so," I extended my hand, "we're still gonna hang out, right?"

"Yeah." Carlo sounded almost surprised by that question. "I mean, dude, it's just a band."

"Yeah, we were friends long before that."

"Call me, tomorrow." He said.

"Okay, you want to maybe hang out this weekend?"

"I don't think I can. We're gonna be practicing with Benji. Get him tighter on the songs." We stared at each other, almost like we both wanted to take one more look. He was free of dealing with me now. He didn't have to worry about what I thought. "Look, I gotta go help those dudes load out, but we'll talk and, seriously Tim, don't even worry about it. It's cool."

"Thanks, Carlo."

"Later, Tim."

He walked away and I got in my car. As I pulled out of the parking lot, I looked in the rearview mirror and I could see Carlo talking to all the guys, telling them that I'd just quit the band. Russ and Benji high fived each other.

Carlo and I weren't going to be hanging out. Not any more. I wasn't going to call him and he and the rest of the Augmented guys weren't going to call me. There was no point in thinking about any tours now. If one happened, I wasn't going on it anyway. I was really out now. More alone than I had ever been.

I laid in bed that night and looked at the Augmented poster on my ceiling. Then I looked at the collage of band photos I'd put together. Pictures of shows, us recording, road trips. Then I looked at a few pictures of Erika and I. One was at a family gathering. The first time our parents had met. She and I were sitting on the couch in her house. I remember being stoked because having our parents meet was a pretty serious thing. Now that picture had been taken at a place I could no longer go. There was another picture of us. I was standing behind her with my arms wrapped around her waist. I kept staring at the pictures of Erika and I. They were the only ones that mattered.

Chapter 39

Garden Grove and Westminster were areas I didn't go to much anymore. I did a little bit when I was younger, especially to Westminster Mall, but for some reason Carlo and I stopped going there and started going to South Coast Plaza in Costa Mesa. Whenever I drove through Garden Grove and saw all the Asian and Mexican places, I didn't even feel like I was still in Orange County. Especially when I passed through a place like Little Saigon. I had never shopped there in my life. There just didn't seem to be anything there for me. The most I knew about it was that Gleaming the Cube starring Christian Slater had been shot there. Where I lived in Fountain Valley (and Huntington Beach as well), these places seemed to be like the final vestiges of how things had been before everything changed. Before areas like Garden Grove and Westminster had started spilling over into where I lived. In many ways, it seemed like the look of the southernmost cities was being pushed closer and closer to the ocean, until they would be pushed out completely.

Of course, it wasn't really this way. It was just the way I had chosen to see things. I guess I just found all of this interesting, because I remembered how these places used to be back in the 80s and early 90s. You really don't notice things are different until they are. But things being different doesn't mean that they are bad. I knew that now, even though I wasn't sure how much I believed it.

I continued to stare at the buildings as we went down Brookhurst street into Garden Grove. Mike had picked me up in his lowered Toyota that he, Johnny and a bunch of their friends had tricked out. He'd had it lowered which "made it easy to drive" he said. The windows were tinted and he'd had a large speaker system put in the back taking up what seemed like most of the seat. Normally, I would have given him a lot of crap about all this. He would've made fun of me and I would've made fun of him right back, but our friendship was different now. A line had been crossed and things had suddenly become serious.

"So you quit the band, man?"

"Yup. No girlfriend, no band, no tour; nothing."

"People are still looking for those guys." Mike glanced at me. He didn't have to say which people because I already knew. He knew that. "They ask me if I know who it is because I know you, but I tell them 'No.'"

"Thanks... seriously."

"They'll find them, you know? They know they're in that band."

Mike continued to look at me after he made each statement because I was being uncharacteristically quiet. I'd been like that a lot lately. I used to always know what to say, or I had a sly comment for every situation. I didn't seem to have that anymore.

"Tim, why you wanna apologize to Quan? You weren't even there?"

"I don't know. Someone's gotta say something, right?"

"Why you? Why not them?"

"Because maybe if I apologize, that'll sort of help buy my friends some time? They'll see how stupid all that White Power stuff is and get out of it." I honestly had no idea what I hoped to accomplish, it just seemed like the bigger risk was not doing anything at all. To talk to Mike's friends, to let them know that we weren't all like that, it had to count for something, didn't it?

"Quan's brother, Nam, he wants to kill those guys, man. For real."

"You think he'll try?"

"Nah, he's a punk. But who knows? People get crazy right?" He wanted me to know that what happened between his friends and my friends would never be forgotten.

"Yeah... I guess they can," I said as an afterthought.

"When are you going away to school?" He asked. The day for me to leave was closer than it had ever been and I still hadn't made up my mind.

"I don't know if I'm going."

"Why?" Mike didn't seem surprised, he actually seemed annoyed.

"I don't know if I want to go away. I don't know what I want to do."

"Your parents want you to go?"

"Yeah."

"And they're going to pay for everything?"

I nodded my head. Mike laughed a little bit.

"Chhhh, if my parents wanted to send me away to school, and they were gonna pay for it, I'd be gone, man."

"Really?"

"Yeah, they wanted me to go away when I graduated High School. I got into some places but they couldn't afford to send me anywhere."

We pulled up to a block of homes that looked like many of the houses in my neighborhood. Suburbs are suburbs, I guess. Two guys sat outside the house we stopped in front of. One was tall and wearing workout type clothes. Next to him was another guy who was shorter. He wore a dark purple windbreaker and dark blue jeans. He had a look about him... like Benji. They were different races but you don't have to be anything in particular to look angry. I stared at the guys a little as Mike turned the car off and took the face of his stereo and put it in a plastic case.

"Lets go, Tim."

"Yeah."

We got out of his car and walked up to the house. For a split second, I wondered if this was a setup. Mike had played nice and brought me here, but now they were gonna jump me. As dumb as that may sound, these guys were Mike's friends. His boys. If they had him convinced that maybe I was there that night... I decided not to think about it.

"What up, Mike?" The tall guy asked. They shook hands.

"Not much, Eddie. Quan's here right?"

"Yeah," the guy in the dark windbreaker said. He didn't look at Mike as he answered. He just glared at me. "Is this the guy?"

I stuck out my hand. He just stared at it so I put it down.

"Yeah," Mike said. "This is Tim. He's cool. Tim this is Quan's brother, Nam."

I followed Mike into the house and Nam and Eddie came in after us.

Asian homes have always seemed different to me. Not that I've been in that many, but there appears to be more of an "older world" feel to them. More of a reverence for the past as opposed to most Western homes which seem fixated on the present. The here and now. It seems like the past has it's place and it's usually not so out in the open, whereas in Asian homes it seems to all run together. The past is just as prominent as the present and even the future. It kind of reminded me of how Erika's house was.

Nam and Eddie sat down on the couch next to Quan. He and a few other guys had been watching TV. The living room had some pictures on the walls and there was a lot of furniture. I could've sat down and probably should've. I just wasn't thinking right. I couldn't remember the last time I'd been this scared. Quan's head was still covered in a large white bandage and he had some bruises on his face. Staring at him, I still couldn't believe my friends had done what they did.

At this moment I realized that nothing I was going to say would matter. Even though I hadn't been with Carlo and the others the night they attacked Johnny and Quan, that didn't matter. I was here now and I was just as much to blame.

"What up, Q?" Mike and Quan shook hands. At any moment, I expected these guys to start beating the crap out of me.

"Hey, Mike." Quan looked at me and then his expression became like everyone else's. For a moment I wondered if any of these people even knew I was coming.

"This is Tim," Mike started. "He's the guy who wants to talk with you."

I stared at everyone. I was here now, I had to do something. For some reason, I started thinking about hardcore. The real reasons for why I'd gotten involved with it. It was different and I wanted to be different, and I had to show these guys that despite what they thought, I was different.

"Look Quan, I'm really sorry about what happened."

"Why you sorry, man?" He stated angrily. "You weren't there, right?"

"I wasn't, it's just... those guys are really confused. They're not racist... you see, we all grew up here..."

"We all grew up here, too! What do you think we're all fresh off the boat?"

Some of the guys laughed.

"No, it's just that our neighborhood has changed so much from how we remember it. I think it scared us. So we tried to do something about it but we did it wrong."

"What are you talking about? What does this have to do with us? We didn't do anything."

"Look, nothing I'm gonna say is gonna come out right, but all my life it seemed like my neighborhood was one way and now all of the sudden it starts changing." I stared at Quan. I had to start explaining things better but how do you explain something that you don't understand? "Look, I'm sorry about what happened. I wasn't there when my friends did what they did, and I don't know everything they said, but we're not like that. My band, Augmented, is not about hating people. I know you guys are planning on doing something to my friends, but it's not gonna help anything."

"Forget this white boy!" Nam yelled.

"You guys are right to do something," I continued, hoping that at least some of them we're still listening to me. "But that doesn't mean you should. It's not gonna accomplish anything."

"They're just gonna keep doing it, man. If not to me, it'll be someone else they get." Quan barked back.

"They won't, I'll talk to them. I'll get them to stop."

"That won't do anything. Where were you before? Why didn't you talk to them before they jumped me and Johnny?"

"I did. I swear. I totally tried."

"So why would they listen to you now?" Nam asked. "If we don't do something they're gonna think we're punks."

"Why do you care what they think?"

"I didn't say I cared what they think. I care what I think and your boys are gonna get messed up!"

"Look at you, man!" Quan started. "You come here with this story, 'We grew up here, things changed, we messed with you but don't mess with us.' It's always the same with you White people. You think you own everything. You think you're better than everyone. We were all born here! We're just as American as you! Why don't your friends come over and apologize?"

"Come on, Quan," I said. I had done this all wrong. I don't know what other way I could have done it, but I knew I had picked the absolute wrong one.

"No, man, those guys could've killed me. They probably would've if they could have gotten away with it. It would have been one less gook in your neighborhood. You come here and expect us to care about what you think? You were scared because there were people that lived in your town that are different than you? You're a racist. You just think you're not because you weren't with those guys that night but you are. You're just like them."

I had nothing to say. This situation had become so uncomfortable I wanted to step back, sink into the wall and disappear. What had I really hoped to accomplish by coming here? I wanted these guys to know that I was different, but was I? I still had things inside me. Thoughts. Opinions. Ideas that were inside my head; that were ingrained in there. Not allowing me to think any other way. They'd been there so long, I had no idea when they started. I just knew how I viewed myself and everyone who wasn't like me. I wanted to say more. I wanted to defend myself but I couldn't. I didn't have anything to defend. Deep down, I thought I was better than everyone in this room. Who were they to yell at me? Maybe I was silenced because I'd finally realized that I wasn't better than anyone? I'd never been.

"Let's go, man." Mike turned to me. I started walking out of the house. He was getting me out of there because he knew his friends. If I kept talking, chances are they were going to beat me up.

"Yeah, get out of my house! Get out of our neighborhood," Quan said.

I stopped and slowly turned around. I looked at Mike and then at Quan. I hoped I wasn't going to start crying. It was hard to talk because I was so nervous.

"I'm sorry, Quan. I'm really sorry about what happened. I'm glad that you're doing better and that you're okay."

I turned, opened the door and walked outside. Mike and I didn't say much on the drive home.

Chapter 40

I really hadn't spoken with my parents after our "talk" last week. Whether it was on purpose or it just worked out that way, I wasn't home when they were or I just wasn't in the same room, or maybe we had decided that we all needed some space? I never told them about the possible Augmented tour and now I was glad I hadn't. It would have just been another argument that didn't matter now, right?

Anyway, when I walked into the kitchen, I was surprised to find my dad sitting at the table having his morning coffee and reading the newspaper. I'd just assumed he wasn't home because the house was so quiet.

I went over to the pantry and started fixing myself a bowl of cereal. I might've made a quick exit except I was really hungry. I could have taken the cereal up to my room but I didn't feel like it. He was my father and despite how angry I was, or had been at him, we had to talk eventually, right?

I sat down at the table and ate in silence. I picked up the newspaper that my mom had left sitting there.

I could feel my dad looking at me so I looked at him.

"I'm sorry about what I said last week," I said. I figured this was as good an opening as any. Lately, it seemed I'd had more and more things to be sorry about.

"So am I," my father said as he folded up the newspaper and put it down.

"Look, I was mad and really confused, but that doesn't excuse what I said and I never should have talked to you that way."

It felt good saying these things. I meant them. I felt humble all the time now. Like I wasn't so fixated on any one thing anymore. I felt like I was more open to things.

"Tim, I was wrong too. I've been wrong."

Been wrong? My father had never apologized to me for anything.

"Look, nobody's twisting your arm to go away. You're more then welcome to stay here and go to school, but your mom and I, we just think it would be a great experience for you."

"I know."

"But if it's not what you want..." he stared at me for a moment, "what I should be saying to you now is, if you have a dream you should follow it."

"I guess I really don't know what I want to do with my life."

"Tim, that's what college is for."

"What if I get out of school, I get a degree in engineering or something, but it's not what I really want to do?"

"So what?" he replied matter-of-factly. I stared at him for a moment to make sure he wasn't kidding.

"How can you say 'so what'? This is my life? My future? This is money you're gonna be spending to put me through school. A lot of money."

"Tim, don't you understand? You'll have a degree. You'll have options. You don't have to get a job in something just because you majored in it. Get a job doing something you love. Teach guitar, do your bands at night, work at McDonalds for all I care. Just try to find something that makes you happy. That's the most important thing."

As we continued to talk, I slowly realized that what had been the biggest hurdle, the biggest barrier, was that I wanted to be treated like a grown-up without realizing all the responsibilities that it entailed. I also realized I wasn't a kid anymore.

I don't know quite when that happened but it scared me to death.

Chapter 41

Going to the mall alone sucks, but it's even worse when you have to go without your girlfriend. Especially when this was a place you routinely went together. Not that there weren't a fair share of pretty girls at Westminster Mall, but all they did was make me think of Erika. All the times we had come here... I tried not to think about that too much because the thought of three years of something being over was too overwhelming.

So I focused my attention on the people in the mall. They all had their own lives, their own problems and I didn't mean anything to them. I was just another person. A nonentity. I wished I couldn't feel at all, simply because I was having one of those days when everything sucked. Losing all your friends and your girlfriend in one summer was a lot to deal with. Things had been up and down emotionally after that talk with my dad, but at least I was back on some kind of normal footing with my folks and that was good. Things may never again be how they were when I was younger but my life didn't have to be so crazy either.

"Hey, Wilkes!" I was broken out of my thoughts by a voice I didn't quite recognize. I turned around to see Isaac and Shayna standing behind me holding shopping bags. It was sort of odd to see them outside of a hardcore show or the Pushing Forth warehouse. They looked like normal people.

"What's up?" I asked.

"Just shopping. You've met Shayna, right?"

"Yeah." I extended my hand and Shayna shook it. "We met at that show in Riverside."

"Yeah, Rusty's Garage. I really like your band's CD," she said. Her voice was softer than I remembered it being. She always seemed sorta tough. I had never spoken to her (other than for a second at Rusty's) but she looked mean.

"Thanks." I looked at Isaac. "I'm not in that band anymore."

"Oh, sorry."

"No, it's cool. I like that record too."

"You should," Isaac said with a smile, "you spent enough money recording it."

"It was all Carlo." I smiled.

We all laughed.

"So what are you doing?"

"Not much, just shopping. What's up with you?" Isaac asked.

"Just buying clothes." I held up the two bags I was holding. "I leave for school in a week and a half."

"So you decided to go?" Isaac was surprised.

"Yeah."

"That's cool. It'll do you good to get away and be somewhere else." He stared at me for a moment after he said that. "Talked to any of your boys?"

"They're not my boys anymore, Isaac. You know that."

"Yeah, you quit. Those guys are so stupid. They keep calling Corruption about taking them on tour. Once I told them about Benji being in the band they were just like, 'forget those guys.' Alex, that kid who pulls orders at the warehouse, he saw Carlo at Blueprint talking about how supposedly some A&R guy from Capitol Records is gonna come see them."

"Really?" I hadn't heard anything about that. My stomach went cold because I'd walked away from that band, but I quickly realized I didn't have any choice.

"It won't happen," Isaac said reassuringly. I must have looked like I needed it.

"Why didn't those guys work this hard when I was in the band?"

"They're idiots, dude." He looked at Shayna to make sure she wasn't bored. Hardcore girls that are "into" the scene are just like hardcore guys, we love to know what's going on behind the scene. Behind the facade of what we see on stage or hear on the records. "It sucks, man. Augmented could have been so big."

"I'm bummed about quitting, but what can I do? I'm way more upset about breaking up with Erika."

"You two broke up?" Shayna asked.

I think I remembered Erika mentioning that her and Shayna had talked at a show, or maybe they talked somewhere else. Anyway, I remember Erika saying that Shayna was "nice."

"Yeah," I said. I hated admitting that we broke up. Mainly because I had felt so helpless during the whole thing. I felt as though I had just let it happen.

"You just got to give her her space, man. You know how people are. She was with you for three years, you don't forget about that."

"It sure seems like she did."

"Are you going to the show Friday?" Isaac was good at changing the subject.

"To see Augmented? I doubt it. Are you?"

"There's this band Conversion that I want to check out. Trial's playing. I was actually gonna split before Augmented go on."

"Really?" I knew about the show but I had never even thought about going.

"Come on, man, go with me. It'll be your last show before you leave. Shayna can't go, you can work the merch booth."

"Dude, Isaac, seeing Benji on stage playing my songs is gonna kill me."

"You're not even gonna see him. We'll bail before they play."

"Go with him, Tim, Isaac needs help. He can't sell all that stuff by himself." Shayna smiled at me.

I looked at Isaac and decided that if I was gonna be anywhere near that show, I was gonna be there with him.

"Yeah, I'll go."

Chapter 42

"Hey, are you guys playing tonight?"

I was standing at the Pushing Forth Records merch booth with Isaac. A young kid had just bought an Adjust 7". They were a new band from Boston that had sent their demo tape to Isaac out of the blue. He liked it, called them and they were on the label. I remember Russ and Carlo not liking them, but then Carlo started hanging out with Isaac more, Isaac gave him a 7" and suddenly Carlo didn't remember not liking them.

Club Royale was packed tonight. It was between bands so naturally loud music, unrelated in every way, shape or form to the scene was blasting over the speakers of the club. I think club owners figure as long as they play something between bands "the kids" will be happy. "I should start wearing earplugs," I thought. I was getting into my role of hardcore elder statesmen. No longer in a band, still going to shows, being in my early 20s... I was having all sorts of stupid thoughts. I couldn't help it, I felt awkward. I was at an Augmented show and I wasn't playing. I was here to sell merch for a band that I was no longer in.

"Augmented? Yeah, they're playing." I finally responded.

"Aren't you in Augmented?"

This conversation was awful.

"No... not anymore."

"Really? Why?"

This kid was starting to get on my last nerve. Being at the show was bad enough, but having to talk about why I was no longer a part of something I had created, with friends I had known forever, was a whole other deal I didn't even want to think about.

"I quit." I gave the kid his change. "I'm going away to school."

"Oh," the kid said as he took his money and his 7" and walked away.

I wasn't Tim from Augmented anymore. I was just Tim Wilkes. Was I nothing without my band?

Isaac was staring at a group of skinheads. He wasn't looking at them with disdain or anything, he just looked at them like he knew who they were.

"Hey," I said.

"Some Sharpees are here." He stated.

"Sharpee" is another term I had heard people use for SHARP skinheads. The name means SkinHeads Against Racial Prejudice. I didn't really know too much about them, other than that they were non-racist skinheads.

"Really?" I asked, looking at them now. "How can you tell they're SHARP skins?"

"Their patches and stuff. I also used to know some of them; not real well. That big one used to sing for that band Terraform."

"Didn't he stab someone when they were on tour in Las Vegas?"

That was one of those hardcore scene urban legends that had been circulating for years. Another one I had heard was about a guy from San Francisco named John Barini, who supposedly is hated for ripping off all these bands he tours with. The weird thing is, I always hear about him continuing to tour.

"I heard something about that. Who knows?" Isaac looked at me. "You know why those guys are here right?"

I nodded my head.

"What do you think they're gonna do?"

"Hopefully nothing."

I heard Benji and Sonya at the bar when I was ordering sodas for Isaac and I. They were both talking and laughing loudly with a group of people. Most of the people around them had really short haircuts. A few had Confederate flag patches on their jackets, while others had "88" written or patched onto theirs. Later, Isaac told me that "88" was a code for "Heil Hitler". H was the eighth letter in the alphabet. "88," "Heil Hitler."

"What's up?" Carlo's voice broke into my thoughts. I hadn't even seen him come up to me.

"Hey," I said.

He looked different. Something about his eyes and his clothes. He was more slicked up tonight. He didn't look like a hardcore singer, like the same person you'd see inside the Augmented CD layout. He looked special, or like he thought he was special.

"I didn't expect to see you here?"

"Why not?" I smiled, trying to lighten the moment. "Just because I'm not in the band doesn't mean I can't hang around, right?"

"I know. I just thought you were over it."

The thing was, Carlo wanted me over it. Not just over the band but the whole scene. I was a reminder of something to him. Deep down he probably hated me and I didn't care because I didn't like him too much anymore either. I don't think I had for awhile now. I didn't like who he'd become.

"Nah, not yet." I said casually. If I played it cool and acted like I didn't care, that would make him even madder.

"You will be." He didn't look at me when he said that. There was no eye contact. He was busy looking around the room, seeing who else was there, who else he could talk to. I had seen him do this to other people before, even to Russ, but he'd never done it to me.

"So Benji is working out?"

"Yeah, he's good. He picked up the songs pretty easily. We're going out at the end of the month."

"Really?"

Augmented was finally going to tour. I didn't feel as bad about not being a part of it as I thought I would.

"Yeah," he said trying to figure out how much this was bothering me. "By ourselves. It's only for like 10 days, up and down the West Coast, but it's more than we've ever been able to do. We then want to go out for a month at the end of November."

"That's winter," I said, realizing it as I said it. Very few bands went out during wintertime. Being in a crappy van with no money was tough for even moderately established bands. Who knew how it would be for a band that had never gone out before?

"I know," Carlo smiled, "we're psyched. We decided that if this can't break us up, nothing can."

"What about getting on another label?"

"We're talking to New Dawn, but with them being on the East Coast, it might take some time. We wanna record something now. We might do a 7" for this new label in Europe."

"That's cool."

"Look, I gotta go warm up. You're gonna watch us right?"

"Yeah." I replied. And I decided I was now. For a couple of songs anyway.

"Ladies and Gentlemen, we are Augmented from right here in beautiful, sunny, southern Orange County!!"

The crowd cheered wildly as Carlo started his opening speech. Isaac and I had been flooded with people wanting to buy stuff during Trial's set, so we were late taking the merch booth down. I asked him if he was sure he wanted to leave, seeing as how there were probably a lot of people who might want to buy Augmented merch and maybe they were waiting to do it after they played. As there were no "ins and outs" at Club Royale, people often waited until after the show was over so that they wouldn't have to carry whatever they bought around with them all night. Isaac said he'd rather "lose money than watch Augmented play."

"Who's the new guy?" Carlo asked, responding to someone in the crowd. He and Benji laughed to themselves. "This new guy is the legendary Benji Walker." A few people cheered, mostly his friends. "He's been tight with Augmented for a long time. This is a man that's truly down for his crimes."

Russ played a short bassline. "Orange County" was now stenciled into his bass in old English lettering. They'd also put up the new Augmented banner before they got on stage tonight.

"Where's Tim Wilkes?" someone else in the crowd yelled. I tried to see who it was, to see if I knew them.

"Who? Tim Wilkes?" Carlo looked out into the crowd to try and find me. Some people standing around looked at me to see what I was doing. It didn't take Carlo long to stop looking. "I don't know, man, he's in school or something now. Anyway, out with the old, in with the new. We're gonna have a good time tonight. You should all know this song, it's the title track off our 12" from a label we're no longer on. This song is called 'All The Way Back.' It's about commitment. It goes out to Tim Wilkes and Isaac Myles for talking shit on us and ruining our tour!"

Augmented began to play and the club went nuts. They didn't sound that bad either. Well at least not as bad as I had hoped they would. I was trying to not be too nitpicky but Benji was very sloppy on guitar. He didn't seem to care though. He was really into it, I had to give him that. The audience sang every word with Carlo. Russ and Benji rocked out together as Adam kept perfect time on the drums. I was really going to miss playing with him the most. Russ and Carlo were good but I think Adam was more talented at his instrument than all of us.

Russ looked at Benji to make sure he was playing the right chords. After a few moments, Carlo turned and looked at Benji as well. I couldn't help smiling. I wondered if anybody else was seeing what I was seeing. Then I began to wonder about what Augmented might sound like if Benji started writing songs?

There were breaks in the song and that's when I noticed some people "Seig Heiling" and raising their fists to the lyrics. Carlo, Benji and Russ raised their fists as well. Like they'd been practicing. I looked at Isaac and he shook his head. He turned around and began to pick up the merch to take out to his truck. I turned back to watch the band figuring we would leave after this or the next song. Although, I had to admit, my reason for continuing to watch them was in the hopes that they'd fail, really mess up badly, and then they'd see just how much they did need me.

Suddenly, a fight started in the pit. I don't know what happened but it seemed like some of the SHARP skins and some of White Power guys had begun throwing punches. They were being thrown by everyone it seemed. People were trying to get out of the pit, but they couldn't. They were just swallowed up as the fighting escalated. The pit continued and so did the music. Carlo had to see what was happening but he didn't tell the guys to stop playing like he always had before.

Isaac and I moved toward the pit to try and help some people and break up the fight. That's when some Mexican guys in the pit grabbed Carlo from the stage and slugged him in the face. People then rushed the stage as the fighting escalated. One SHARP skin decked Benji. He went down so hard I thought he might be unconscious. People started going after Russ but he threw down his bass and ran out of the club.

As people were moving all around me that's when I noticed Quan, Johnny, Eddie and Nam. They had a few other Asian guys with them. Johnny pointed toward to the stage. He was pointing at Adam.

"ADAM!!!!" I screamed.

I began to move toward the stage but was knocked into the pit area. I fell to the ground and people started punching, kicking and stepping on me. Everything was happening really fast. Too fast for me to do anything about it and too fast for it to really hurt. I tried to cover up and for a moment I thought I was going to be killed. That this brawl was never going to end.

Out of nowhere, Isaac started to pull people off of me. He was like some unbeatable figure you see in a war movie. Bombs and gunshots happening all around them and they're oblivious. People started to advance on Isaac, but as they did I think they realized who they were moving toward and they seemed to stop. I somehow got out of the pit area. That's when I realized that my shirt was ripped, my nose was bleeding and my left eye was starting to swell. I had blood all over my shirt, arms and hands where I had been punched, kicked and stepped on. I looked for Adam on stage but I didn't see him anymore.

People were now trashing Augmented's equipment. They stomped on their guitars, pushed over their amps and kicked in Adam's drums. As I made my way outside, I saw some people rip down the Augmented banner from the club wall.

I ran out into the parking lot where there was a huge crowd already. More people continued to file out the door behind me. The closer I got to the crowd, the more I realized that other fights had broken out as well. Some people were trying to keep the peace, but this situation had become something more than a few people fighting at Club Royale. I heard glass breaking, bodies hitting against cars, then I heard sirens and saw the blue and red lights of police cars and ambulances. It was surreal to be witnessing all of this.

I started moving again. I had to get out of this parking lot; away from Club Royale. As I dipped between some cars I stumbled a bit and that's when the Augmented van flew past me, missing my body by what seemed like inches. The force of the van spun me around some as it screeched out of the parking lot.

I looked back at Club Royale again. At all the people who were standing outside. It was amazing to realize that my band had had the power to bring all these people together and also push them so far apart. Everything was heightened. All the lights and sounds. If I stopped moving I felt like I would collapse.

I took off running as fast as I could.

I had slowed up my pace a bit (I was never much of a runner) but I kept it pretty steady, and it didn't seem like it took me that long to get where I was going. The quietness of the suburban neighborhood was eerie, especially compared to the scene that I had just witnessed at Club Royale.

I got up to the house and knocked on the door. I tried to not have my knock sound frantic, but there was probably no way around that.

"Hello?" A voice called from inside.

"Mrs. Lopez? It's Tim." I started breathing even harder now. Harder it seemed than when I'd been running.

It was only when I heard Erika's Mom start to open the door that it dawned on me how I must look. I was breathing heavy and I still had blood all over me.

"Tim, what happened?"

"Nothing, ma'am. I'm okay. Is Erika here?"

At that moment, Erika came downstairs. She was in her pajamas. No matter what she wore looked beautiful. She always did.

She stared at me and I realized that if she walked away now, she was gone. I'd have lost her forever. I couldn't let her go. I wasn't going to let her go. I had been confused about a lot of things but no longer about this.

"Tim?" She was surprised to see me.

"Erika, I'm so sorry."

I walked into the house and put my arms around her. I was crying now. Thank God, I was crying. I had broken through myself. I was totally vulnerable to the person I needed; to the person I loved most in the world.

"I love you, Erika. I'm sorry. I'm so sorry about everything. I didn't mean any of it. I was wrong. I love you so much and I'm so sorry. I love you, Erika."

I squeezed her tighter. I had broken through to myself and I had to break through to her. To let Erika know everything. I continued crying when she hugged me back. Then she started crying as well.

"I'm so sorry about everything. I'm so sorry..." was all I could think to say and I continued to say it; over and over.

She whispered in my ear that she still loved me.

Chapter 43

A little less then five months had passed since the incident at Club Royale. Erika and I were still together and if I had any say in the matter, we were going to stay together. I secretly hoped to marry her after I graduated college, I just needed to tell her that. Being away in Indiana was very difficult, but I called her everyday and we wrote lots of letters and emails. I did pretty good my first semester. I got three A's and one B. The B was in Calculus. I did everything I could in that class, but I could never break out of the 80th percentile. Oh well, at least I'd made some friends. There were a bunch of hardcore kids and some ex-hardcore kids (or post hardcore is what I think they were calling themselves now) who went to the school. There were even some local shows with bands that Augmented had played with when they were on tour in O.C.. I guess people really liked our album. Isaac said we had sold about 10,000 copies but after word got out about the Club Royale show, the sales really nose-dived.

I had let my hair grow out a little bit. I sent Erika some pictures and she loved it. I still dressed pretty much the same, though I don't have such an aversion to collared shirts. I have more friends now who aren't straight edge (mainly guys who drink and smoke pot) but I still am.

People talk about peer pressure and stuff, but I've never really felt it. I think it depends on the person. I'm proud of the fact that I don't drink and someday, if I want to, I will. But not right now.

I came back to Orange County for winter break. I mainly hung out with Erika and my parents. Being away had certainly spiced up things between Erika and I. It was like we were trying to make up for being apart and trying to make up for when I would be gone again. I visited Baha Burgers once. Mike and I didn't talk too much about what had happened at Club Royale. Carlo and all those guys got what they deserved. That was that.

One morning after breakfast I saw in the O.C. Weekly that Augmented were going to be playing some "21 and over" club I had never heard of. Right then, I knew they were in trouble. As a band we had had a rule that we would never play any "21 and over" shows. Yet, here Augmented was going against that. It didn't surprise me, as they had pretty much turned their backs on everything hardcore was about as far as I was concerned, but for some reason I still felt like I had to see them. At least I planned to anyway, unless something better came up.

"You're still playing guitar, right?" Isaac and I were in the Pushing Forth warehouse. He was silkscreening some Function t-shirts as we talked.

"Yeah, when I can. It's like I said, school kicked my butt last semester. There's no way I could've done it here. Too many distractions."

"You should keep playing, Tim. You're too good to stop."

"Some guys I met in the dorm, they're more into punk and ska, they wanna jam, so we'll see." Even I didn't know how into that I was. I personally can't stand ska music.

"You should do it. Record some stuff and let me hear it."

"Why? You wanna put it out?"

"Why wouldn't I?" He smiled. It was funny how I felt so much closer and more in touch with Isaac then I think I ever did with any of the Augmented guys. We were tight, don't get me wrong, but I saw myself being friends with Isaac regardless of if there was a hardcore scene. "It's not gonna suck, is it?"

"You never know," I laughed. I watched him screen another shirt. Bringing up the band was inevitable. No matter what, I still cared. "I see that Augmented is still playing."

"Yeah, I guess. After that riot show those guys have been having a lot of problems getting booked."

"So they didn't get on another label in New York or anything?"

"Nobody's gonna put them out. Not after they admit to supporting that White Power crap. Carlo says they're going to start their own label, but you know those guys."

"Yeah." I did know them. They could do a lot of stuff. Would they do it was the question?

"They're not gonna do anything." Isaac eyed me after he said that. "It's sad, Tim. Augmented could've been so big but they messed it up. They cheesed out."

"I see that they're playing tonight?"

"Yeah," he laughed. "Morgan's. It's pay to play."

"It's also 21 and over," I said.

"Yup, all those guys drink now."

"Yeah... Adam quit a while ago."

"I don't even know who's in the band now. Are you gonna go to that show?" Isaac smiled

"I might."

Then his smile turned to surprise.

"Why?"

I looked around the warehouse a bit before I answered.

"I guess, because no matter what happens, Augmented will always be my band. Even if it's not the band I remember."

Chapter 44

"Erika called," My mom said as we sat at the table eating dinner. Things between myself and my parents (especially my dad) had really improved. There seemed to be more of a respect. Me for them and them for me. Who knows how it would have been if I hadn't gone away to Indiana like they wanted me to? The fact is, I went because I wanted to go and I was happy they were happy with me. I was also really happy that I had gone.

"Yeah, I'm gonna see her later tonight."

"How's that working out?" My dad asked.

"It's working out as well as it can with us living half the country apart." I smiled at him. I no longer felt like every answer I gave him was the wrong answer. He no longer acted like he wanted a different one.

"What's it like being back after the first semester?" My mom asked.

"It's fine... but it's different. I mean, I've lived here my whole life. Now, I'm somewhere else and that place is supposed to be my home, but I don't have any history there yet. Then I come back here and I have a certain... pride, I guess, for my new home."

"Are you homesick already?" My mom smiled.

"No," I said. "Not yet."

"Are you going to take the same load of courses next term?" My father asked.

"Actually, I'm thinking about taking more. I only took 12 units this last semester. I think I'm gonna try and take 15 this next one."

"Don't you think that might be too many?" My mom was always concerned about me taking on too many things at once.

"Nah, I can always drop a course if it is. You two should be happy. The more units I take, the quicker I get done, the less money you'll have to spend."

My mom looked at my dad.

"In that case, take 20 units next semester," he said with a laugh.

My relationship with my parents was different now, but in a good way. It had been a very hard lesson to learn but things change. Everything does. That's just how life is. I don't think things are ever meant to stay the same.

To be like how they are when you're a kid.

Chapter 45

Morgan's was a dump.

Believe me, I was trying to root for these guys, trying to imagine that Augmented had something of what it used to have, but it was all gone. Morgan's just seemed like a large room with a PA system. An excuse to sell alcohol. It was dark and there were about ten tables with chairs set up. Outside there were about 10 people, many of them much older than any fan I ever remember attending an Augmented show in the past. Inside there were about 20 more. I guess 30 people showing up to a 21 and over show on a weeknight wasn't too bad. The thing is, Augmented had usually played to over 200 people no matter what day of the week it was.

There were about 10 people standing in the pit area, though most of them just seemed to mess around, pushing each other, giving the band the "metal" sign and yelling things at Augmented as they played or in between songs. We had played some shows like this when we were starting out but we always knew it would get better. Now? This is what Augmented had become. I was more embarrassed for them than anything else.

I really felt bad for Carlo. He had been my best friend. I was closer with him than I was with anyone else in the band. He was still into it. Still dynamic, but nobody here seemed to care. They were indifferent to him, and by the comments the "crowd" yelled you could tell they didn't take this "little kid" seriously.

Benji was way out of tune. Russ was very sloppy and the person on drums seemed like he'd started playing a month ago. Even the Augmented banner that they had been hanging up was now crooked and dirty. What made all of this even worse was that they were playing my songs. It all sounded dissonant and jumbled. Did these guys even practice? How could Carlo let things get like this?

I saw Sonya and Deborah sitting at a table, smoking and drinking together. As tough as Deborah came off, I had always thought she was pretty. Now, she just looked older. They all did. Then I wondered if I looked that way? Maybe I was being too critical? Maybe Augmented could "bring it all back" as people in hardcore sometimes say?

I doubted it.

"This next song is a new one, not like there's really anybody here that would know our new ones from our old ones." Carlo said in between songs.

People yelled things at Carlo. Hardcore and punk shows were different. At punk shows, people seemed to have more of a "show me" or "impress me" attitude. Whereas at hardcore shows, as homogenized as it was, the audience seemed to root for the band, hoping that they were going to be good. That's probably why I had always liked those shows better.

"We're gonna be releasing a new 7" on our own label, Augmented Records, next month." Carlo continued. More people made comments. "This is the first song off of it; it's called 'Youngblood'."

Carlo was desperately trying to make a connection. To speak to someone in the club. To anybody who might still care about this band. To anybody who remembered who they were. He had never had to work this hard. He wasn't used to talking through a PA system and getting no response.

As Russ started a sour sounding bassline the rest of the band came in. It all sounded like noise and I decided to leave.

I was driving down the street on my way to Erika's. As I drove, I noticed that in the area of Anaheim that I was in, there was a lot of graffiti on the walls. People of different races and ethnicities were walking around. Mostly Mexicans in this part of town. I didn't stare for too long. I didn't care anymore. Who was I to judge anybody, right? We could all be here. We could all live together.

I came to a stoplight and I picked up the Augmented CD that had been laying on the passenger seat. I looked at the front cover, remembering when Carlo first came over with the picture out of some National Geographic magazine. Two people fighting in some foreign land. He'd given it to Isaac and he'd made the cover look really good. The Augmented logo ran down the side. I opened it up and glanced at the lyrics and "Thank You" list, but what I really wanted to see were the pictures of me, Carlo, Russ and Adam. All of that stuff seemed so long ago now. Starting the band, getting popular, Isaac putting our first 7" out, then the CD, everything that happened last summer...

I took the disc and put it in the player. I was somewhat relieved when the first song started and it still sounded like I remembered Augmented sounding. Why I thought it wouldn't I had no idea, I was just happy. This was the real Augmented. Not that group I had just seen at Morgan's. This was how people would remember us. Alive. Energetic. Standing for something. Only hardcore music has that feeling. That sound. At least to me it does.

For a moment, I was brought back to what it was like to play in that band. To be a part of something special. Then I realized, I would do a new band. It might never be like Augmented but I would do one. I had to. Playing music was a part of me. I just had to get everything together again.

The stoplight turned green and I started driving. I was on my way to meet Erika, the girl I loved. It was going to be great to see her. To talk to her about the past, present and the future. To think about them together even if we didn't always agree on everything. That was part of the fun. It was going to be great to think about all that stuff.

I had already thought too much today about my summer of hate.

The End